'A masterly novel of grief and conflict ... Audacious and moving... What it means to be civilised and behave with decency are questions raised throughout this fine novel' *Sunday Times*

'*Land of the Living* is a poised and carefully crafted novel of powerful, submerged emotions, taking an under-explored aspect of Britain's war and ending in it something graceful and strange, mythic as well' Allan Massie, *Herald*

'Revelatory in many ways, shining a light on the darker aspects of war' Nilanjana Roy, *Financial Times*

'A landscape of arresting beauty and extreme violence ...Vivid, illuminating and unbearably tense, this is a masterly meditation on trauma, on beauty, on the idea of home and on the limits of love' *Guardian*

'The quiet power of Georgina Harding's novel lies in how she conveys with such bruising lyricism the way language fails.... *Land of the Living* is a moving testament to the battle that starts once the fighting has stopped' *The Times*

'Her *Land of the Living* is as wise and haunting as its predecessors' Lucy Hughes Hallett, *New Statesman* Books of the Year

The Gun Room

'Georgina Harding's novel is the finely tuned work of a writer exceptionally at ease with her craft and a testament to the power and poetry of clean and disciplined prose … *The Gun Room* focuses minutely on one man and in doing so it tells a deep history of the many men who, having seen war, struggle to be anything but soldiers' Sadie Jones, *Guardian*

'The narrative flits between past and present in an impressionistic manner; facts and character emerge slowly. The dreamlike quality is heightened by Harding's sharply observed prose, conjuring up with great intensity the claggy English fields, Vietnam's pockmarked delta and Tokyo's ordered suburbs' *Sunday Telegraph*

'A captivating, superbly written novel about the impossibility of escaping from the past' *Mail on Sunday*

'A powerful novel about war and its aftermath in memory … The narrative attends to its people with delicacy and detail. Stubborn and painful memories are evoked in a nuanced understatement, and the frequent inarticulacy of the characters only intensifies the power of the prose. The writing is allusive without ever losing lucidity, and the whole is beautifully orchestrated. It is an excellent novel' Abdulrazak Gurnah, *Financial Times* Summer Reading

HARVEST

Georgina Harding

BLOOMSBURY PUBLISHING
LONDON · OXFORD · NEW YORK · NEW DELHI · SYDNEY

BLOOMSBURY PUBLISHING
Bloomsbury Publishing Plc
50 Bedford Square, London, WC1B 3DP, UK
29 Earlsfort Terrace, Dublin 2, Ireland

BLOOMSBURY, BLOOMSBURY PUBLISHING and the Diana logo are
trademarks of Bloomsbury Publishing Plc

First published in Great Britain 2021
This edition published 2022

A catalogue record for this book is available from the British Library

ISBN: HB: 978-1-5266-2506-9; PB: 978-1-5266-2510-6; EBOOK: 978-1-5266-2508-3;
EPDF: 978-1-5266-4293-6

2 4 6 8 10 9 7 5 3 1

Typeset by Integra Software Services Pvt. Ltd.

Printed and bound in Great Britain by CPI Group (UK) Ltd, Croydon CR0 4YY

MIX
Paper from
responsible sources
FSC® C171272

To find out more about our authors and books visit www.bloomsbury.com
and sign up for our newsletters

Two definitions:

Mau Mau: *possibly from Kikuyu; name for militant nationalist movement against British rule in Kenya. For the British of the 1950s, a word associated with terror and atrocity.*

Mā mā: *Japanese; an everyday word meaning so-so, OK, comme ci comme ça.*

He sent her a photo in the spring, of daffodils and trees without leaves, and the house behind the trees. She couldn't see much of the house in the photo, only a stretch of brick wall and a tiled roof, and two lines of windows reflecting sunshine. The point of the picture was the brilliant yellow of the daffodils in the foreground that was meant to tell her that, whatever England was, it was not always grey.

He was standing in the midst of the daffodils. Grinning and holding out his arms.

Come and see me, he wrote. Just that, in soft pencil, on the back of the photograph.

Already she had imagined the place he came from, from things that he had said before. When she got the photo she imagined it differently. When she finally went there it would be different again. Nothing, when you saw it, was quite as you imagined.

And people, she would think, wasn't it like that with people? That they were not as you imagined, or even as you remembered them? Or so it seemed to her, after that summer. That people weren't as you thought they were – or even, you weren't quite who you thought you were yourself.

Once she was there of course she knew how it was, so she forgot, or almost forgot, all she had thought it would be before she came, from whatever he had said and whatever she had made out from the photo. Jonathan's house was big, and old, and many people had lived in it. She was aware of that as she had never been aware of it anywhere else. She had a sense there of others in the past who had lived in those rooms, other women before her opening the doors, touching their fingers before hers to the rail of the stairs. Almost all of the people that she had known until that time lived in quite modern houses – except for her grandparents, and their house dated only from around the end of the Meiji era, so although it looked old it could be no more than eighty or ninety years, and her grandfather had been born there, so she thought that it was never lived in by any other family. Her grandparents' house was nothing like so old as Jonathan's. This house was hundreds of years old. It was bigger than any house that she had known, with passages and cupboards and an attic that nobody entered, spaces in it that were never touched, not like a Japanese house where you could reach to every corner. And they wore their shoes indoors. That was only a little thing, but it was the sort of thing that it took time for a Japanese to get used to. There was old dark furniture, a smell peculiar to the place that was both dust and polish, a still dry smell of indoors that told you how the people who lived in the house spent most of their days out of doors, out of the house in the clear air outside, and there were worn rugs here and there on worn wooden floors, glowing Persian reds and blues, and in the bedroom where she slept, a thin faded one that slipped beneath the feet. The floorboards had big cracks between them. When she took off an earring and dropped it, sitting on the antique stool before the table with the mirror, she was afraid for a moment that it had fallen through one of the cracks. Beside the lion's paw that was the foot of the stool. She wondered if there were more earrings down there in the dust, earrings and hairpins and coins, wedding rings even, that had slipped down and been lost beneath the boards maybe for one hundred or two hundred years. Or longer.

It was only a little pearl stud, one of a pair that was the first present Jonathan gave her. She thought them a bit of a cliché and not really her style, but he had been sweet and shy with her then. She wouldn't have liked to lose it.

She had asked him to tell her about his home, many times. She wanted to know so that she could know him better, so that she had some world to fit him into, that he came from, so that he had some dimension deeper than being just an Englishman who had come to Japan, who turned up one day at the language school where she worked, and got a job teaching English because he was English and someone else had left, and that was all the qualification or identity that was needed in Tokyo in the 1970s, Englishness. She did not yet understand what a freedom it was to him to be just that, an Englishman who had come to Japan and had no need of other identity. Sometimes a language teacher, sometimes a photographer, whoever he felt like being, with his leather jacket and his hair (that had been cut too short when he first arrived) left to grow a little long, quietly outside of it all. She would come to think that it was that quality that made him a good photographer; what seemed like the freedom in him, that he could be one person or another, the way that he could hold back but at the same time seem to empathise, both close and distant at once, as if he could look from outside and yet reveal things about a person as if he had seen inside them.

She didn't even know about the photography, to start with. Not until he had been coming and going for some weeks. She had been aware of him only in the background, a slim dark-haired Englishman who appeared as the replacement for a blonde Canadian girl, and who was nice enough, and attractive in a subtle way, and seemed to do everything OK, and came and went at the right times. They did not get talking until there was a problem with a student, a grown man who just disappeared, and she saw how he was concerned about this man. Sometimes it was like that, attraction, as if a person opens a door, and suddenly you look in and they're interesting to you. The two of them stayed late in the office trying to contact this man and then when they left they went to a nearby tempura restaurant to eat, because it was late and they were hungry. They never did know what happened to the man – maybe something bad but maybe nothing bad at all, maybe he had just moved on without telling the school or paying his bill – but because of him they ate tempura and Jonathan got talking, telling her about his travels. Doors opened onto doors. She thought that he had spoken a lot about himself, and then they said goodbye and she got on the subway train alone, sitting there in the carriage with the evening still alive in her head, as the train ran and stopped and the passengers came in and went out at the stations, and she realised that he had talked almost all about other people's lives and places, not his own.

What is it that's so important for you to know? he would say. You know me, all that matters of me. But she wanted to know more. How had he come to be in Japan? Where had he come from? Why? She thought, that's how it is when you fall in love with someone. Not only the first day, but always. You want to know what it is that makes you love them; if it is only the surface, the dark lashes about his grey eyes, his smile with that reserve in it, that becomes so warm in those moments when the reserve goes, or the feel of his skin, tanned from hot days they spent that summer at the beach in Izu, his body taut as he stretched back on the sand; or if it is more – and she told herself it must be more, mustn't it, if she and he were anything or to amount to anything – that it must be who he is inside, where he comes from, his story. (Or maybe it wasn't. Maybe there was no more than the moment. Or an accumulation of moments that she or the two of them had strung together, one way or another. The tempura restaurant, Izu, a garden they went to see, the mountains in autumn, so many everyday moments in the city that were different because Jonathan was there and he made her see them differently. Maybe that was what Jonathan, the story of knowing him, taught her. Maybe a man, whoever it is that you love, is no more than what he appears to you to be at some particular moment against some particular surroundings. How he then moves, in those surroundings, at your word or your touch. How he makes you see them, and yourself. Maybe he can be no more to you than that, and your love has no existence in any time but the present. Maybe love is only a passing thing. Unless you choose to make it otherwise. Unless you work on it in the memory, call-ing it back, making – fixing – the story. Maybe that was why Jonathan took photos, fixing all those moments to carry forward into the future.)

She said to him once, Tell me about your family.

She had known him only a short time but already he had met some of her family, her mother's parents, in the old house in Kamakura. They had been to Kamakura sightseeing, walking round temples in the rain.

He had a mother and a brother, he said. His father died in a shooting accident when he was seven. (Not the truth, then. Only something close to the truth. He would not tell her the truth until much later, when he was about to go home to England.) They had a farm. His mother had kept the farm for them – at least, for his brother who wanted to farm, if not for him.

Oh, she said. She did not quite know what to say. She just had an ordinary Tokyo life. Nothing bad had ever happened to her and she had never even been on a farm. Didn't your mother marry again?

I guess she didn't meet anyone, he said. There weren't so many men for her to meet, out there in the countryside.

So she asked him to tell her about the farm. The house where he grew up.

He said the house was a big, rambling old farmhouse. His voice was slow, a little distant, though he lay close beside her. It was the first time they had spent a night together. They had come back from Kamakura and gone to his apartment, in a tatami room bare of things and with the windows open to what seemed like those days' unending rain, and made love there. They had the conversation the next morning when they woke. Or maybe pieces of it came at other times. At least, this was how she would remember it. Talking while their bodies were soft with the sex and the rain, as if they might melt, one into the other.

What's 'rambling'? she said. It was a difficult word for a Japanese to pronounce.

'Rambling' meant that the house had no plan, and rooms ran into rooms as it had been extended, piece by piece, over centuries, as the owners had bigger families or made money and wanted to be stylish. There was a symmetrical brick front, added in the eighteenth century, but a muddle of earlier rooms behind. And there were two staircases, one main one and an old steep back staircase for servants.

You have servants? she said. It was a puzzle to her, the England where he lived.

Oh no. Only the house had servants once.

It sounds grand.

Not so grand. All sorts of houses had servants in those days. A cook, or a maid to sweep and clean, make the fires, I suppose, carry water in jugs up those stairs, do whatever it was maids did.

She could not picture it. Do you have any photos to show me?

No.

If you're a photographer then you should have photos to show.

Not from home. I left home to take pictures of other places. I didn't bring pictures with me.

Oh.

He had brought only the camera. His eyes. As if that was all he wanted to be when he travelled away from home, eyes. (He used his eyes and his lens. On her. On Tokyo. On all the places where he went. Before he came to Tokyo he had used them in a war. And he had run away from the war to come to Tokyo. He did not tell her that in the tempura restaurant. She had to know him a long time before she learnt about Vietnam, so well hidden he kept what he had seen. Even when she knew that he had been there, it was some time more before she saw the pictures he had taken. Jonathan was trying to live only some moments and not others, the present moments and not the past ones. It made him complex, much more complex than he had seemed at the start, her Englishman. Elusive. Maybe that was a part of why she was in love with him. But also it kept her at a distance.)

You have all those other photos. Don't you have any of your family? Your mother?

Why should I bring photos? I know who they are. I know what my home looks like. I don't need photos to remember them by.

You might have brought them for me.

Why, he said, and rolled over towards her. Their faces close, eye to eye. Breath to breath. All they could see was each other. They could hear rain soft outside, the occasional movement of wind chimes. Why should I bring somewhere else with me? Isn't here enough?

There can be one moment in the year, Claire said, turning back to the girl even as she led her out into the garden. One moment, she said, looking back, speaking clearly as one speaks to a foreigner, one moment when everything falls just right, the irises still in bloom, the roses just coming out. Some week at the start of June, so long as the weather is kind.

The girl said, Then I am lucky to come here just now.

Yes, it's perfect now. Last year we had a wet start to June and it was all ruined by the rain. These old roses can't bear too much rain, the wet gets in and the petals spoil and begin to rot even in the bud.

The daffodils were long gone. There were roses instead. When Kumiko stood where he had stood to take the photo, she could scarcely see the house for leaves.

It was late in the day so the topiary and the hedges cast their shadows across the lawn, black and geometric before the tangle of flowers. The garden was still, the stillness accentuated by the thin song of hidden birds.

9

Only the insects moved, and a last flurry of pale butterflies, or a first one of moths, as if their wings were all the weight the air could take besides the scent of the roses; and the two women, one half a step ahead of the other. Jonathan was standing at the French windows. She did not want him to join them just then, she wanted a few moments alone with this girl. Soon they would sit down to supper. She had it ready in the oven, keeping warm. And the table was laid. They had only to wait for Richard to come in, then the food could be brought out, the salad dressed, water poured.

Let's go into the garden, she had said. Just until Richard comes in. It's such a nice evening. She thought, Richard should have been back by now. It was rude of him not to have come in sooner to meet Jonny's girl. Rude to keep her waiting when she must be tired after her flight.

Oh, the girl had said, so smoothly and lightly, I would love to see your garden.

Really, this Japanese girl was quite disarming. Not what she had expected.

Have my mother show you her garden, Jonathan had suggested, when they were on their way in the car. He had come to Heathrow to pick her up. It was six months since she had seen him. She had been a little afraid of how it would be when he was back in his own country. There had been a few phone calls, but international calls were difficult in those days, with echoes and time lags. She would hear her own voice coming back to her, which sounded like the voice of a schoolgirl, more Japanese, more accented in its English than she had realised, and then the other one, an Englishman's voice that surprised as if she had never heard it before. Heard the voices waste expensive minutes speaking of the time and the weather. Put the phone down with a sense of what had not been not said. Then a photograph came in the post, bright with daffodils, and written on the back of it, Come and see me. And she held it and planned, put it on the shelf where she looked at it for months. She went to work in the morning and came back in the evening, alone to her one-room flat. It was still there, beside the teapot, propped up between the teapot and the bills, the thought of Jonathan but also of the adventure, of doing what he did when he came to Japan, going away not just for a holiday but for longer. There were other letters. At last she called and they spoke again. She said the name of an airline, a flight, a time. She had bought her outward ticket but kept her return open. She was taking a great step out into the open. She had savings. She had left her job and she was going to England, and then the two of them would go travelling, all of Europe before them. I'll come and meet you, he said, I'll be there. (So was she going out to the known, or the unknown? Somehow, she wanted it to be both, the man she knew and the unknown place.) Now and then on that long flight, she wondered if she would recognise him, when she landed. If he would recognise her. Why she had gone all that way to see a man she might not recognise. But he was there at the barrier, when she walked through, looking, looking first at faces that seemed like his but not like his at all. He was standing there, real, known. Present. His touch, the smell of him. His voice without distortion or echo. Even his clothes, clothes that she knew (and that were also the past), that they had bought together in Tokyo the summer before, that looked quite worn-out, but he was English and Englishmen liked to wear worn-out clothes. Then they were in the car. They were driving through England. It was not so very different, at first. She had wanted it to be entirely different. It could have been anywhere, at first, from the car, only a place of cars and motorways. And then when they left the motorway and were driving in the countryside she saw the villages, the trees and fields, green and soft beneath the changing sky. He said that they'd had a spell of lovely weather, that it was a good time to come. They talked a lot at first, in the car. Once they were on those country roads they didn't say so much, only as they got close to his home Jonathan talked about his mother.

She's put you in the spare room, I hope you don't mind. (She did mind. She minded very much. She minded the distance that was put between them, from that beginning.) Mum's a bit old-fashioned about things like that, a bit out of touch. But she's looking forward to meeting you. Let her take you around the garden, she'll like that.

He wanted to please her. He wanted her to please his mother. She understood that. He wanted the two women, his mother and his girl, to meet and talk in the garden, two women walking, and he would see them from the window inside, these pieces of his life running one alongside the other.

It had been easy to see that she was Jonathan's mother. She was small and slim and dark like him, quite dark she thought for an English person, a pretty woman still. Her face was lined, from being out in all the weather, she thought, in the garden and the countryside, lines about the eyes and grey in her hair, but she moved briskly as if she was younger; precision in her movements, a little sharp and tight.

They walked out from the house across the lawn. Jonathan stood at the window. No need to come with us, Claire had said in her crisp clear way, and he had said no, fine, he'd seen the garden so many times; though he didn't turn away, he didn't seem to be wanting to do anything else.

There were double doors that opened into the heart of the garden, onto flagstones, a little area where there was a table and chairs, and then onto the lawn and the flower beds and the hedges. It was late in the day so there were long shadows. There was this one moment in the year, Claire said, stopping and turning to look at her, when the garden was its best. And Kumiko said then she was lucky to be there.

Claire smiled, out there in the evening sunshine, a neat little English smile that went quickly away, that was like the smile of an Englishwoman in some old movie. (But also like Jonathan's smile, so many of her gestures like Jonathan's.) It was perfect now, Claire said. Kumiko saw that her hands could not resist breaking off a dead rose head as she spoke. She did not even seem to notice that she was doing it.

The girl spoke English well, but with slight pauses where she looked about or her hands moved as she sought a word. What she said was expressed very simply. Claire couldn't tell if this was because this was specific to her or because she was speaking English, or because this was the way that all Japanese girls spoke.

Charles de Mills, this rose is called. It's one of my favourites.

It's beautiful. An English rose.

This one isn't English, actually, this rose is from France. Many of my roses are French. People don't think that. People think this garden is classically English, but

13

it isn't really, not the plants at least. Or perhaps it is, she might have gone on, it was, classically English, just because of that, because the plants came from everywhere, because the mild English climate was so tolerant of plants from other parts of the world whose climates were more extreme, even here in Norfolk, in the east, where it could be so much colder in the winter than in the west, and because the English were tolerant of the way they grew, unlike the French who might have grown all of the same plants but made their gardens so much more formal. But she didn't say any of that. She let her words fade. Perhaps it is, she just said, classically English, looking at the tangle of plants, and left it there. The girl was tired after her flight. One could see that. Tact then, not rudeness, to walk on a little in silence.

She looked like a pretty little doll, Claire had thought when Jonny came home and showed them his photos. Or was that just a mother's resistance to her boy's foreign girl? And this girl wasn't just foreign. She was Japanese. Her son had been away three years, and had spent much of that time in Japan, writing her occasional rare letters from there that said that the cities were vast but the gardens were lovely, and when he came back he had shown them his photos; and now this girl had come to visit them, suggesting that she was important to him, that she wasn't just some girl to be known and loved and photographed abroad and then left behind, this Japanese girl with a bright face, who was yet so obviously tired after her long flight. And here she was, speaking to this girl, making conversation, letting conversation pause, noting how the greenfly gathered on a rose shoot, and how composed the girl seemed, despite her evident tiredness. She didn't really know anything about the Japanese, she thought; only what Jonny had said, in his letters and since he had come home. She had been used to thinking of them mainly as the people whom her husband had fought in the war, hating them even, for that – though Charlie had said so little; what knowledge she had was drawn mainly from what others said, others who had been in Burma or been prisoners, or more often others who had known other people who had been there, as no one who had actually been there seemed to say very much. Slowly over the years, over the time that Jonny was away, she had come to revise her understanding, to see that his Japanese were different from theirs, to accept that the one thing didn't necessarily connect with the other, the history and how things were now. Even so, that didn't quite dispel the distrust. Though she had to admit, really it did look as if the two of them had had a happy time, Jonny and his girl out there in Japan, this pretty girl always smiling her wide open smile, on the beach or in the park or in the mountains or wherever it was they went.

Now that they had met she saw that the girl was neither quite so pretty nor so doll-like as in the photos. Her nose was perhaps too small, mouth too wide, for prettiness, features somehow too irregular for a doll. Women like Claire had been brought up to regard themselves and their kind critically. To think, if her legs weren't her best feature then should she wear her skirt so short? But the brightness of her expression made up for much of that. She managed some brightness even as she shook away a little yawn that showed how tired she was. She put up a hand to stifle the yawn, shook off her tiredness and looked about her some more. How long have you lived here? she was asking. Did you make all this garden yourself? Since I was married, Claire said, and yes, she had made the garden, over the years; it was amazing to think that almost everything that was in it now she had planted herself, so little remained from before, things that she had planted become trees, views cut off, others created, the place quite transformed. Even Charlie would scarcely have known it now. Do you have a garden in Japan? she asked, and the girl said no, she had always lived in an apartment, though her grandparents had a garden, her grandparents had an old house in its own garden, not so big as this one, in fact very much smaller, but a very nice garden all the same. Again the girl yawned. Let's go in, Claire said, have supper. We'll start without Richard if we have to. You must be so tired after your flight.

She was awake a long time the first night. This was not surprising, after the flight. She had never flown long-distance before. She felt the night grey in her head, not black, never quite black. The night was grey and the room where she did not sleep was spare and the house where so many people had passed in the past sounded of emptiness even though Jonathan's mother and his brother were asleep in the rooms along the passage, and Jonathan himself asleep where he had slept through his childhood – and the dog downstairs, which was a new dog, Jonathan had said, that his mother had got while he was away, not the kind of dog they used to have, big golden dogs, retrievers, but a spaniel, black-and-white and long-eared, which slept in a basket in a corner of the kitchen. She had an idea that the emptiness she heard was not only inside her jet-lagged head but also the wind in the hollow of the chimney above the fireplace in the room. And that was black. In the winter, she thought, in the past when those others had lived in the house, there would have been a fire burning, smoke filling the chimney in the nights, and inside it would be black from that, soft and black from soot; but now in the summer the chimney was empty. The wind brought the sound of the clock from the church across the fields. The sound came through the open window and down the black chimney also. She put on the light and saw that the time on her watch was still the time in Japan. One a.m. in England, by the clock. Nine in Japan. She corrected her watch and lay awake some more.

She thought about the day. She thought about the past that was all around her in the house, and was connected to Jonathan but not connected to her; the past of people she had never known. They had gone for a walk that afternoon, she and Jonathan and Claire. They had lunch, and then they took her around and showed her the village and the church, tall and white in the sunshine that came through its long windows, and close to the church, the Hall, at the end of a long drive. Claire said that the family used to live in the Hall. And then in the 1930s Jonathan's uncle had sold the Hall and come to the farm, and brought with him to the farm all the stuff that they had in the house – not everything from the Hall of course, she said, because the farmhouse was so much smaller, but whatever was best and most valuable or meant something to the family. I imagine the rest got lost along the way, she said. Sold or burnt, she said, disposed of; you know how these things happen. But how was a girl like Kumiko supposed to know a thing like that? She pictured a bonfire in the fields, of furniture, of whatever it was that a family did not value, old brown cupboards and chairs, and broken picture frames and books and bookcases and dishes, lost between the Hall at the edge of the village and the farm-house in the countryside, flames and an upturned table, and the hedgerows and the church behind.

She didn't hear him coming, only the door when it opened. He knew how to walk those old floors without making a sound.

Did you always walk around this house at night, she whispered, without anyone knowing?

Was that what he had done as a boy, creeping down the passage, down the stairs? So that his mother didn't hear, his brother didn't hear.

The stairs have carpet on them now, he whispered back. It's much quieter since the carpet was put down.

They were like naughty children, excited to be doing secret things in the dark. Giggling as they tried to be silent, biting fingers, hands over each other's mouths. It was so long since they had made love.

Are you happy to be here?

Now I am.

And she was at that moment, everything about her foreign and new, even though it was so old, except for the feel of his skin and the smell of him against her.

He was gone before she woke up. (Why could he not have stayed until she woke, she thought, so that she might wake beside him?) It was six a.m. and light like day. The church clock sounded, a minute ahead of her watch. In Japan it was afternoon already. She went to the window and pulled back the curtains. There were no other houses to see. There was no one to hear, not inside the house or outside of it. There were birds singing. She felt she was the only person anywhere. She was a city girl. She had never had that feeling before, that she was the only person in the world, getting up out of bed and drawing the curtains onto a bright day where no one was. She stood at the window looking down at Claire's garden. There was the lawn, and there were all the flowers, and behind the flowers a hedge like a wall, so dark that it was almost black at that time of the morning with the sun low behind it. The hedge was high so that if someone was walking on the other side he wouldn't be visible from the house, it would be way above his head. And he would see nothing of the garden or of the people in it. He would have to stand a little bit back even to see the upstairs windows of the house. She saw Richard there, out in the field. She didn't know if he saw her looking down, her face behind the glass.

Beyond the hedge was Richard's farm. The fields were all one shade of green, stretching out a long way. It was a duller, bluer green than the grass in the garden. Jonathan said that if she stayed long enough she would see them turn to gold.

*The lovely garden of Joséphine
de Beauharnais*

I want lots of flowers, she said to Charlie. Colour. I want masses of colour.

The garden lay white under snow. It was 1947, a cold winter that seemed to be meant to cauterise the recent past. When Claire looked out there was no distinguishing any more between the surface of the garden and that of the fields beyond, smooth and white to the grey horizon. Even the line of the fence was erased where a drift had swept against it. She had woken before him. Gone out into the snow. Now he had come out to join her.

Roses, lupins, irises, dahlias. Delphiniums, I love delphiniums. Peonies, big deep red ones. What else? Rhododendrons and azaleas. Can one grow rhododendrons here?

But you don't know anything about gardening.

It was true. Those were about all the flowers she knew, apart from ordinary little flowers like daisies and forget-me-nots, which never found their way into London florists'.

I'll learn. I can begin to learn before the snow melts. As soon as the snow goes I'll start work. I'll get Billy to help.

She hadn't lived in the house long enough yet to make a mark on it, so full it was of the family past, but the garden was clear out there, blank now.

It'll be wet, Charlie said, when all that snow melts. You won't be able to get into the ground, you'll have to wait a while.

Well, I can start planning, darling, can't I?

She brought down Uncle Ralph's gardening books from the shelf in his study that had become Charlie's study, moved them into the sitting room, moved a table before the window where she could see as she planned. She took some sheets of paper, white and plain as the snow outside.

Again then they went out, the two of them together into the snow, paced the white ground. They left their footprints first in straight lines like geometry across it, recording the length and breadth of the lawn from the house to the half-buried fence, making the notes that she would transfer to the sheets of paper; then pacing the distance to the trees, the position of individual trees and shrubs, Ralph's long-neglected border. They might have been treading the foundations of a house they were to build, young marrieds building a life anew for themselves.

What a mess we've made of the lawn now!

When they looked back the footsteps seemed to have lost all order, jumbled, criss-crossing as if there had been a gang of children playing. Or dancing. Charlie's laugh made her feel warm in the cold. Almost as if he had touched her, skin to skin, beneath all the wool that they were wearing.

Then his voice ironical, a serious look. It's not all playing, you know. Gardening's science too.

Do you think I don't know that, living with you and all your talk?

She had been married to a farmer long enough to know that first she would have to learn the soil and what liked to grow in that soil. There were magazine articles with pictures of trees and flowers, and there was the Gertrude Jekyll, but most of Ralph's books were dry. *Sanders' Encyclopaedia of Gardening*. Catalogues on herbaceous plants and shrubs and climbers, manuals on pests and diseases and the pruning of fruit trees, all in tight text with the barest of illustration. A larger book with engravings, about Joséphine's garden at Malmaison which Ralph had perhaps visited at some time before the war. She put herself to work as she had not worked at anything before. The snow had been beautiful at first, but it lay too long. The house closed around them. She planned and planned. Charlie fretted that he could not himself get onto the land, and now she understood his impatience. The melt happened so slowly. Snow turned to slush and then froze again. Even when the snow was gone the ground held on to the cold and then the wet.

The first thing she had Billy do was put in the yew hedge. She had intended just a defining line, a piece of form in this landscape which had so little form. She did not imagine that the yew hedge would grow as tall as it eventually did. Only the very great gardeners could imagine such things, she would think in years to come, the Capability Browns who could see into the future.

If the farm was his to make, then the garden was hers. She made the boundaries, as if to claim some space back from him, some ground that would be her own and separate from all the rest of the land in which the house stood so plain and exposed. She would wrap the garden in hedges, a hedge of yew to the front and side of the house, to the east and south, to claim herself back from his space; and when he was gone she let the hedges grow tall to limit the sky. She made it in spite of him and because of him. But with him too.

She planted the first of the roses the following winter, not long before Richard was born. They came bare-root from the nursery early in February. Richard was due in March.

Are you sure you should be doing that?

It was awkward, digging with that big belly sticking out in front of her.

Why don't you wait till Billy comes? He can do that for you.

She thrust the spade into the ground again but the impact of it shot through her. She stopped, straightened, put one hand to her back, handed him the spade.

Charlie dug the holes then, two spits deep, and she unwrapped the plants from their hessian and newspaper wrappings, untied the strings and loosened the tangled roots, shaking out pieces of the still-damp soil of the nursery from which they had come. He put in a little muck at the base of the hole, as recommended in *Sanders' Encyclopaedia*, and then she knelt and bent over her big belly and spread the roots across the broken soil and filled back in with a trowel. Then to the next, Rosa mundi to Charles de Mills. One after another, they planted the roses all that late winter's afternoon. The day was one of those sudden mild ones, and they had noticed how the light lasted, how spring was on its way. As the sun lowered it caught the yellow patch of aconites beside the drive and made them shine.

Are we done now?

No, there's one more. Roseraie de l'Hay. As the sun dropped it became cold. Her fingers froze even within the leather gloves. That pain came in her back again.

Later she would think that it might have been because of the roses that Richard was born two weeks early.

But it was a good moment for Richard to be born because Charlie had time for them. Wet weather, days of incessant rain, and Charlie was in the house. He built the fires in all the rooms, and for the first week or two her mother came to stay. She had barely needed her because Richard was an easy baby. He slept and woke and fed and slept, some separateness or containment to him, behind his blue eyes that would become bluer as the weeks passed. The house seemed a sure and safe place, with them all there and the lights on and the fire burning, and the rain outside. There was a man who had visited them just the day before she went into labour, someone who knew Charlie from India in the war, and he had left suddenly in the night. When he had left she had the notion that he had taken away some danger from them, that Charlie's heavy winter mood had lightened. But perhaps that was only the effect of the baby coming. That he was happy, for those days at least. She remembered how his hands quivered as he first took the white bundle from the midwife, though they were such big hands that he might if he was more sure have cupped a newborn in one alone.

Then her mother left, and Charlie went back to his work after the rain had stopped, and she was alone in the house with the child.

They had been married almost two years. They had been wary of having children too soon. There had been so much to do, coming to the farm when Ralph needed them, establishing themselves, learning the life. Yet she had felt from day to day as she moved about the house and he moved about the farm that there was a space about them waiting to be filled.

She had thought that a child would fill the space but now he was there it seemed to her that the space had turned to water. That distance she had known between herself and the world, which had been the dry emptiness of the rooms where she had moved each day, the flat fields, the length of the gravel drive, had become a lake, a still grey lake. Now when she moved there was that slight resistance of water, and ripples spread out across the lake, slowly widening and smoothing, almost disappearing before they touched the shore. She woke in the night and fed the baby. She fed him again in the peace of the mornings when finally he slept quiet and long. In those formless lengthening spring days after he was born she had the sense that she, he, the two of them, were floating. An island had formed about them. And Charlie, for all his love, was a visitor to the island. He was one of those others, coming across, holding out his big hands with the smell of the mainland on them. He carried something from outside to her and the child, something separate, apart, that kept him apart in the present, that might yet have been a piece of the past.

Outside, on the shore that she could see from the window, holding the baby to see through as-yet-unseeing blue eyes, the gulls followed the plough. Even when the tractor was out of sight the birds made their trail in the sky beyond the young hedge, white over the brown soil. When Charlie came in the smell he brought with him was earthy and dark. The smell within the house it seemed to her was white.

In the whiteness, the baby slept. She watched, and saw his tiny being quiver all of a sudden as if he was not quite yet of this earth, not even of the island but of the air some inches above, between land and sky. Gravity seized him, deep in his guts, and he woke and cried.

Claire was up a ladder, tying a rose. Kumiko came and stood beneath. Put out her hand to the ladder to hold it steady.

It's all right, she called down. I do this all the time.

The white rose had grown right across a bedroom window.

I just have to tie in this rose.

Claire had lengths of cut string in her pocket. She took one out and held it between her teeth. Once she had the offending stems in place she took off her gardening gloves and did the tying with bare fingers.

When she came down she stood back to look at it. Such a good rose, this one, Madame Alfred Carrière. Isn't that a nice name? Like someone you might know.

Some of her roses, she said, were in the garden of the Empress Joséphine. She told the girl then about Joséphine's wonderful garden. How Joséphine came from Martinique in the Caribbean, and how when Napoleon deserted her – she did not quite explain why, assuming that she had more knowledge of European history than a Japanese education would have given her, not thinking that she might know only the famous names, but not who they were or what they did – when Napoleon was gone, for whatever reason, she had her garden in France made exotic with plants from her tropical home and from all over the world. Joséphine made a life for herself, Claire said. As a woman must. She made the garden, and had plants brought to her from everywhere. Even when the French and the British were at war, ships came through carrying plants from places the British ruled, though the British Navy ruled the seas. And Claire showed her all the French roses in the garden and told her their names. Duc de Guiche, Duchesse d'Angoulême, Belle de Crécy, Comte de Chambord, Charles de Mills. She pointed out the roses gaily, as if there was a party of French courtiers all about them, some great colourful party at a château, music and fountains playing, perfumed courtiers flirting among the flowers, hiding behind the bushes she had made, shaped bushes that were the same dense dark green as the hedge. Not that all of these roses were in the garden at Malmaison, she said. Most of them had in fact been bred later, but bred in France and often from varieties that Joséphine had first brought to the country. They came to one with big deep pink petals. Zéphirine Drouhin, she said. Definitely not one of Joséphine's. A much later hybrid. A bit vulgar for Joséphine, she tended to think.

The girl's eyes were on her, listening, half a smile on her face. She knew she was going on rather. Her sons teased her for that, for rambling about her roses, and here she was, putting her nose to fine blooms like pink petticoats. Was that why the girl smiled? Despite herself, she was beginning to warm to this girl.

Since you're here, perhaps you could help me carry the ladder in.

The ladder was too heavy for her. She had had Richard put it out. Last time she had the ladder out, it was days before she could catch Richard in a spare moment and get him to bring it in. That sort of thing happened too often, when there was only herself and Richard in the house, that things weren't finished because Richard was too busy; the ladder lay abandoned on the lawn, and the grass beneath turned yellow for lack of sunlight.

How polite the girl was, carrying her ladder, listening to her talk about roses. They always said the Japanese were polite. She found herself saying things to her that she hadn't expected to say, opening up a little eccentric- ally, so rare it was to have a sympathetic presence in the house. She was aware that sometimes she talked about her roses as if they were people. Women, always. It seemed to her that roses were feminine, even those that had men's names. She had fallen in love with one or other of them, from time to time. Perhaps the more so because she lived in a world of men.

I was a Londoner when I came here, you know. I didn't know the first thing about gardens. But it was something one could do, I suppose, when one was alone, when the boys' father was out on the farm. I learnt from books at first, made a grand plan, planned it all on paper and planted it out, or had Billy plant it out for me, but then the boys came along, and then for some years I was too busy with them to do much more. It was only later, when I was on my own, that I really began to learn.

After he died, she might have said. As if something from him had passed on to her. The touch of the soil. Awareness of the weather each day as it dawned.

One learns, she said instead, as one goes along. She said it lightly, glossing over the memory of how hard the learning had been, how many mistakes and setbacks and losses, how many little lessons there had been, and how she had faced them, one after another, teaching, toughening herself as her hands toughened with the work. One plants, she said, and then one turns away. Things grow. Or don't. And then one wonders why.

She would garden all of the day until she had no thoughts in her but her work. Go in at dusk, surprised once she was indoors at how late it was, because she hadn't noticed as long as she was outside working. She would eat, run a hot bath, lie in it and scrub the dirt from beneath her fingernails. And when she went to bed and closed her eyes, her head was still full of the things she had done in place of the thoughts, her hands on the soil, the soil itself, the green piles of weeds she had pulled, the forms of roots, the anaemic whiteness of bindweed drawn up endlessly from deep underground.

One watched, she had said to the girl, and slowly, one learnt. One watched the bare soil to see the first leaf appear, uncurl and stretch and become itself, identifiably the leaf of that plant that one had planted and not some other; one watered, tended, transplanted; one watched to see it flourish. And when leaves discoloured one learnt then that there was too much water or too little, or that certain minerals were lacking in the soil, or that there was fungus or pest, just as Charlie had on the farm, Charlie who had walked the crops and plucked leaves and budding heads of grain and regarded them in the sunlight. One learnt the names of chemicals one could use, names that were as sonorous sometimes as the names of the plants, harsh modern chemicals at times, the kinds that they used on the farm, but then as she discovered the harm in them, going back to older remedies that the farmers would have scorned. And other small things one might do. How one might run one's fingers up a tender red rose stem and crush the green bodies of aphids. Or scrape the scale insects from the hard undersides of bay leaves. Or go out at night with a torch and pick off caterpillars. One learnt that the mice had eaten the roots of the rhubarb through the winter. Or that it was the pigeons that had eaten the shoots of the beans – wishing then that Charlie had been there, to shoot the pigeons, the thought breaking through, that they might once again cut the breasts from the pigeons and fry them for supper on a bed of freshly picked salad. (And if they were to open the crops of the birds as they prepared them they would find shoots there, green as they had been torn from the plant, not yet digested.) One learnt that some plants were temperamental. Some that flourished in the summer could not take the cold of the Norfolk winter, the cold of the air or the wet of the soil, which was worse in some parts of the garden than others. One learnt where the frost pockets were, and where was most sheltered. One saw the plants that made it through and those that didn't, the salvias that lasted only a couple of winters and found a third winter one winter too many. Some deaths were obvious. Some one could not fathom. A clematis, for example, could wilt all of a sudden over the course of a few gentle days of summer – or perhaps the problem was not wilt at all but only snails or caterpillars eating round the base of the stems.

And then, she had said, and then one wonders why. The girl was waiting for her to say more, her eyes wide, her little rounded hands open at her sides. If she had said any of that, how could she be expected to understand? She saw that she was not making conversation easy for this girl, who her son was in love with, who seemed really a pleasant enough girl and had come such a way across the world to see him, and was probably about the age that she herself had been when she first came here to live. Hardly any older than she was herself when she married Charlie, she too coming from elsewhere, though only from London, not so far but it too another world, in a way. But this girl seemed so sure in her youth. Open. Carefree. She could see why Jonny liked her so. She did not know that she had ever been so free.

It was late in November when Charlie died. Richard was ten years old. The roses she had planted so soon before he was born were tall bushes, with red hips on them and still a sprinkling of yellow leaves. The hedge stood above her head. Yew grew so much faster than one thought. Or perhaps it was time that went so much faster. Billy had given the hedge a last trim in September so that its lines were sharp for the winter. Now he wanted to clear the borders beneath it, rake out the debris and cut back the dead herbaceous growth. Billy always wanted to make the garden tidy and straight. Let's leave it for the moment, Billy, she said, when she saw him wheel out the barrow with the shears and the rake. She could not bear that year to see the plants disturbed. After all, the dry stalks and seed heads looked so beautiful when there was a frost. She had noticed, in previous years. She had seen the magical appearance of the garden in the first frosts and then regretted Billy's pruning, the logic that said that it must all be cut down and covered over. She had never put voice to her thought before. Let's leave it, at least until the year's turned. She wanted it still, time stayed; even a day like this one, with the sky so grey and the garden so limp and brown.

Billy stood behind his barrow. But we'll be needing to mulch, madam.

Yes, of course we will. She spoke crisply now, as if his words had woken her up. She knew that she must learn to be crisp on everything. It was up to her, everything up to her, now that Charlie was gone. Let's wait till February, she said, that won't be too late, will it? And she had the thought, wasn't there perhaps a purpose to all this dead stuff anyway, that it was cover against the winter?

Billy took his time. She could see how he was considering her, her youth and her predicament, her inexperience in the face of all that was so shockingly set before her. It was Billy who had first found him, who had brought the fact and the dog home. Who had placed his coat over the body, which was why he was wearing Charlie's coat now, since she had given him one of Charlie's coats to replace that one. And the hat he wore, had that been Charlie's too? She was no longer sure. Tweed caps long worn had a way of blurring into sameness. Sometimes it seemed that Billy shared more with her than anyone now. His face was red from the cold, a dewdrop glistening on his nose. But Billy had been to war, the first one if not the second. There were things Billy knew more of than she. No, madam, don't reckon as that'll be too late. And he started to wheel the barrow back.

But, Billy—

Bent to the barrow, he stopped, looked up.

As you're here now, then you might just rake up the leaves from the lawn.

There were so many leaves. He had raked the lawn already, only a week or two before, but it was covered again. The leaves must go on falling until all of the trees were bare.

In the fields Charlie had prepared, the winter wheat was growing.

The stalks came up fine at first, like hairs from the brown tilth. When she stood close in the field she could barely see them, but only from a distance and where there was an undulation or a dip in the surface and the colour accumulated into a green sheen. As the days passed and the crop grew, it angered her. The emerging green was so sharp. Nothing in the landscape should be so sharp and bright this time of year. This was a time of grey and brown and ochre. Black, even. It angered her that the stalks germinated and came up so bold when everything else died back around them. That a man could have sown and not stayed to see his seeds grow.

It was wrong. There was cruelty in it, in planting then. He should have waited until the spring. Or if he was to do what he was to do, not planted at all.

She asked Billy if they had always put in the wheat in October. Billy was old and knew these things.

Billy shrugged. Well that'll depend, madam. Depend on when harvesting's done. When there was only horses doing the work, harvesting might not be finished till November. If there's wheat still standing then you won't be drilling, will you?

No right to it. No wrong. Only practicality.

That was what she must learn. Practicality. Put the pain aside. She must find a man to do the work that he would have done. A man to manage the farm. Talk to him like a man, walk the growing fields with heavy feet, though the green hurt her eyes.

One learned, she had said to the girl, as one went along. And when things went wrong, one wondered why and learned some more. So much she had had to learn, and so quickly. There should have been a fallow time, a long fallow time when nothing changed and nothing grew. But the world had been impatient about her, the farm, the men asking her questions, making demands even though she could see the hesitancy, the difficulty in them each time they came to the door. And the boys kept growing. Richard grew out of his clothes and Jonny grew into them; Richard's clothes bought large for growing room but soon become too small, passed on to Jonny who was a much smaller build anyway and on whom they seemed to wear out before they ever quite came to fit.

The night was cold. She stood with her back to the tall black hedge and looked at the house in which her boys slept. They had a routine by now, the three of them, that had been made through the dark nights of that winter. She had put them to bed before seven, read them a story until they were asleep, then closed the book shut and laid it on the table between their two beds, gone out and downstairs, leaving the door open a crack despite the cold of the house, the light on in the passage so that the room would not be dark. Leave the light on, Mummy, won't you? Jonny always said. This was new, this winter, that he wouldn't let the house be dark. Of course I'll leave the light on, I always do. She had bought a night light to put in their room but Richard said that it kept him awake. The light in the passage was a compromise. Night, night, see you in the morning bright, she had murmured, in case one of them was still awake behind his closed eyes. Or was she saying it for herself, to carry herself through to the morning? She had gone down-stairs to the kitchen and eaten a little of what she had made for the boys earlier, and spooned what was left into a bowl and covered that with a saucer and put it in the fridge, and cleared the table, and washed up, and tidied, moving this way and that across the kitchen with the radio for company. With only the three of them living in the house the clearing didn't take up enough time. Then she had called the dog and taken her out. This was one of the things Charlie used to do, taking the dog out before they went to bed. Out the back into the yard. She could see what a fine cold night it was. The stars were bright already. Often she would only stand on the doorstep until the dog had done her business, but this night she had taken her big tweed coat down from the hook by the door, and her hat and gloves from its pockets, and gone outside herself, closing the door on the house and the boys and the warmth. She had walked past the windows of the empty kitchen where the radio still talked, across the lawn that was already crispening with frost.

The hedge was tall behind her, just so much above her head. The dog had run into the flower beds, rustling between the stalks where there must have been some other creature out there besides themselves, or the scent of one at least. The house stood plain against the night sky, the Georgian façade on this side like that of a doll's house, the window at the end of the passage above the stairs lit bright and a glimmer filtering from the boys' room. They were there in their beds, exhaling their boys' breath as they slept. She would look in on them later, tuck them up and breathe in for herself the heavy smell of their sleep. But for now she was cold outside, looking in. As if she might freeze into a pillar before the hedge. She must find herself, pull herself back in, go inside, call the dog in, go back into that light and out of the frost.

Enter the doll's house, lock the door and bolt it, take off her coat, put fingers through her hair where the hat had pressed it down. The radio was still talking. Switch it off. Turn out the lights. Go upstairs. Tuck in the boys.

Hover some moments at their door with the light from the passage behind her. In her bedroom, again, a radio. The Home Service, which talked until midnight and then played the National Anthem and closed down. Reach out into the crackle of emptiness and switch that off too.

Nothing then to mark the passage of the night. Broken sleep tailing away into precarious day. Coming downstairs, putting the kettle on, stoking the Aga. (The stoking had been Charlie's chore; really she must modernise now that she was on her own.) Waking the boys. Daylight.

The rush of getting them up and off to school.

Two coats.

Two satchels to be found and checked.

Jonny's turn in the front; Richard in the back.

The day grey. Some of these days were never fully light.

She could quiet their squabbling by having them practise their times tables. Seven sevens are forty-nine. Seven eights are fifty-six.

Behind her, Richard's voice boomed out. She could let him lead the chant now, sure before his younger brother who became hesitant as the numbers got higher. Nine nines are eighty-one.

Avoirdupois now; weights, pounds and ounces. Even Richard having trouble here. Sixteen ounces, one pound.

She must drive with care on these narrow lanes, reversing to let the milk lorry pass. Measures. One thousand seven hundred and sixty yards, one mile.

A brief silence then, only the sound of the car, the low brick building of the school coming into view, other cars and children ahead of them. She would keep the engine running as they got out and went in the gate, yet holding still a minute longer than was necessary.

Until there was no one else to be seen, the doors on the school shut, the yard empty but for the coloured lines painted across it, the other mothers gone. There was only herself, a woman in a stationary car, exhaust clouding in the cold air.

She took the journey home slowly, seeing the frost disperse from the grass and the plough. She noticed the catkins in the hedges which had just begun to loosen and show yellow. It was February. Almost three months gone, the worst of the winter. At a bend in the road she came upon a deer. She was going so slowly there that it was easy to stop. A roe deer, caught in fright, in the centre of the road. She saw the stilled poise of its body, the alertness of its ears, the black depth of its eyes. And what was she? A woman in a car, the engine turning over, exhaust. Was it woman that the deer saw or only car, for all that she felt its look within her? Then it turned its solemn head and slipped sudden and fast as spilled liquid through an opening in the hedge. She watched it run across the bare field in a series of fluid bounds, the white fleck of its rump rising and receding across wet brown soil. And a thought came to her. When Billy comes, she thought, I shall ask him to clear those dead stalks from the borders. Have him clear them now, before the spring. A second deer appeared from behind an oak and crossed the road and entered the field after the first. The brown of its body like that of the other was made distinguishable only by its movement against the plough.

While Billy cut she made a pyre of the stalks and burned them. They flared up and were gone in no time, so long they had been standing.

The borders lay open for the new growth. She could see the blades of bulbs already rising, even the thicker shoots of herbaceous plants emerging, brown shot with red and green, life within them, unravelling, pricking through the clumps.

———

When she walked the fields the mud weighed on her boots. If the mud clung to your boots the ground was too claggy to work, the men said.

Men spoke spare words. Words with weight and texture to them.

They made her aware of her own apparent lightness. But she was not light inside. She would be hard and heavy as they. Perhaps she always had been, though she had seemed light. Stronger than they knew. She put on lipstick in the hall mirror before she went out to face them. Put a scarf over her hair. Tied it beneath her chin. Spoke those words, firm as they did.

She must speak men's words to her boys. Plain words, that was what boys needed.

Boys will be boys, people told her. She looked fragile, even if she wasn't. The scarf, the lipstick, didn't convince. People gave her their advice. You have to be tough with boys. She couldn't argue. She had no brothers. She didn't know boys before she gave birth to them.

They use sticks as guns. You'll never stop them doing things like that.

She did not like to see them using guns. She would like to have had no gun ever again in the house. But they lived on a farm, and farms had guns and farm boys learnt to shoot, and her boys were boys on a farm and she must bring them up to be like other boys.

Cowboys, holsters at their hips.

Where are the Indians?

Behind the trees.

Usually Richard made Jonny be the Indian but Jonny did not like always to be killed.

There was Jonny tied to the walnut tree, rope wound about him, handkerchief stuffed as a gag in his mouth. He shook his head at her. She removed the gag. He looked afraid. No, put it back, he said, urgency in his voice. So she did that. Boys would be boys. She mustn't meddle. Was he Indian now, or cowboy? Horse driven away, tied up beneath a cactus in the desert. Left to rot in the sun.

She found the two of them lying across the drive waiting for the postman to come in his van. We're dead, Mum. We're not here, only our bodies. The two of them were lying with eyes closed and arms crossed over their chests. You can tread over us if you like.

The postman screeching to a halt. Off with you, lads, want to get yourselves killed?

That's how boys are, the other mothers said. Boys fight. Boys play chicken. Boys play dead. Boys leave their clothes on the floor. Break things. Fall out of trees. You can't stop them being boys. As if the two of them were a single phenomenon. Wake boys, feed boys, send them to school. Fetch them from school, have them do their homework, put them to bed, the two of them in the same room as since Charlie died they would not sleep alone. Richard said that he needed Jonny to tell him stories so that he could sleep, and Jonny generally did what his brother wanted. And after she had said goodnight Jonny began his stories, his little voice piping up over his older brother's silence. Don't listen, Mummy, these are boys' stories. They won't work if you listen. No, Mummy, I know you're standing there behind the door. You're listening. You have to go away.

Only ten minutes, boys. I'll time you. Then you have to go to sleep.

Often Jonny's voice would hush only when he heard her footsteps coming back up the stairs.

Jonny says Daddy killed a tiger. When he was lost in the jungle.

Jonny says Daddy was captured by cannibals. That's not true, is it? If he was captured by cannibals then he would have been eaten, wouldn't he?

Darling, I don't know what Daddy did.

You should have asked that man.

Which man?

Daddy's friend. The lizard man. The one who came to lunch.

_____

Jack Hussey was the only person she knew who knew where he had been. Who might have known what she didn't.

Jack Hussey had come from Africa in June, the year after. He said that he hadn't taken a leave back in England in years. He had been thin and dry the time he had come before, the one time that she had met him; and he was the more so now. His hair was almost gone though there was still a biscuity colour to it, his face sallow and deeply lined, his hands freckled and long and bony. He had a way of stretching his fingers out in the sunshine, which she thought might have been to do with the onset of arthritis.

It had been Jonny's idea to call him the lizard man. Jonny knew about lizards because someone had given him a book about them. He said the man had to go into the sun to warm up. That was why he came in the summer, even though he was Daddy's friend and the summer was ages after Daddy died. He had to wait for it to be warm.

He had some colonial position up in the hills in Kenya. He said that it suited him. He had been in India before, in the other hills of Nagaland, in the wilds of Assam, and that was where he had met Charlie during the war. That had suited him too, according to what Charlie had said; the highlands, the natives, perhaps the loneliness. All she knew was that he had loved the place but left it heartbroken after Independence. He had come to see them – Charlie, rather – soon after he came back to England, shaken by it, undecided as to where he should go next, considering retirement, leaving their house unexpectedly almost as soon as he had come to it.

Do you know, she said. Did Charlie tell you, the day you left, the time you came before, was the day Richard was born?

He smiled at that. Oh, I had no idea. Then perhaps I did the right thing after all. I left so suddenly, I felt rude doing that, but perhaps it was meant. And as it turns out I haven't been back to England since.

I'm sorry I couldn't have come to see you sooner, he said. This was the first long leave I could manage. I'd like to have been at the funeral.

Jonny was right, she thought. It would have been too cold for him in November. The damp chill. A lizard still on the doorstep, seeking the one pale ray of sun. Freezing when the sun left the cold stone.

His expression of condolence was conventional but heartfelt. It was only that the hands that closed around hers were chilly, even in the English summer.

You were married to a good man.

They drank a sherry before lunch. That seemed the right thing to offer, only later she remembered that he had drunk whisky the time he came to see Charlie, and rather a lot of it. The boys were playing out on the lawn.

Your older one has a look of him.

Yes, she said.

They talked of this and that. How things were in England nowadays. How lovely the garden was beyond the open window. After lunch, she said, I'll take you round, if you like, if there's time before your train. They talked plants. He said that he grew many of the same things in Kenya; had done in India too, in fact. You could grow all sorts of things up in the hills. Roses he thought grew better in Kenya than almost anywhere else. Ah, she said, with a kind of disappointment. She had thought Africa was all exotics, flame trees and jacarandas. Yes, we have flame trees, but no, it's not all like that, then he paused and said, I'm sure it's not like you think, and his faded blue eyes met hers and he wasn't speaking of gardens any more. There was one thing she wanted to ask, which she thought that he, perhaps, of all Charlie's friends and acquaintances, might have been most able to answer. She didn't have to ask it.

It wasn't the Japs, he said, putting the green sherry glass down on the side table before they went to the dining room to eat. Charlie didn't have a hard time with the Japs.

She thought of Charlie as he had been in those November days the year before, seemingly absorbed in the work of cultivation, the scent on him of soil and diesel, no sign in him that she could see of any other purpose or preoccupation. And yet ...

No, of course, I suppose I knew that, she said; though that wasn't quite true, perhaps in truth she had allowed herself, almost as a platitude, a commonplace, to blame it on the Japs. I know, she said, it wasn't as if he was a prisoner or on the railway or anything. Yet somehow she had blamed the Japs. It was easy just to think what others thought, to hear the weight and cruelty in the word as others spoke it in those days, and let its implications carry. To leave it at that, in a simple monosyllable. No need to think further, deeper, for all the decade and more they had lived together.

He had nightmares, you know. He used to wake in the night.

Other women she knew spoke of that, that too something of a commonplace. It was what happened to so many of the men when they came home. So many of the men about them, recovering from the war.

A stalled moment then, before she called the boys and they went to eat. The glasses down on the table, they standing before they moved to the door. Things she wanted to ask but perhaps they were things that couldn't have been told.

I was never in action, Hussey said. Though I saw quite a bit of the consequences. Some men took it hard. But really, none of it is quite what one thinks.

He stood back to let her through the door first.

There was something else, though, wasn't there? She might have asked and he might perhaps have told her, but what would she have asked and what did she want to know? It was history now, all history, the war over, he gone, the two of them here, the place where he had been, India, gone too, in a way, no longer that place where he had been, that he had seemed to hold in him.

There was something else, wasn't there? Out there where you were? That was what she wanted to ask. All she said was, Come again, as she drove him back to the station. The boys had to come in the car with them as there was no one at home to mind them. You must come and see us again, next time you're in England.

He said that he didn't have much connection with England any more.

At least the boys weren't fighting. So often they fought in the back of the car. She took a look behind her. They had the windows wide open and were leaning out, each on his own side, feeling the wind and the land passing. It was so green this moment of the year. Was it as green, she wondered, where Jack Hussey lived? If he could grow those plants then she supposed it must be, though the Africa she imagined was quite other, vast and brown and open to a blue horizon. She drove on, came to a crossroads, waited for another car to pass. There was so much that she had not asked this man, that she sensed he might have said, if she had asked, and now he was leaving.

So you'll stay in Kenya?

For the foreseeable future.

But is it safe? I read these awful things in the papers. She had read of an uprising, atrocities, white farmers killed in their beds. It's frightening, she said, what's going on.

It's not what you think, he said. Again, he was saying to her, it's not what you think. He spoke forgetful of the boys in the back of the car. She supposed that he wasn't used to being with children, didn't know how much they picked up in adults' talk. I know what they say here at home, he said. But it's not us they're killing, it's each other. Blacks being killed, horribly, and blacks killing blacks, not whites. And there's worse. There are terrible things going on, that don't get into your papers at home.

Terrible things, he said, looking out of the window at the green land passing. Things you see that you never forget.

Then they were drawing into the station and he was buying his ticket and his copy of *The Times*, and since they were early they were all of them going onto the platform to say goodbye, as if he was some favourite long-loved great-uncle. She thought how they had spent more time talking of gardens than of what mattered. The other thing. Not only the horror. That she thought she could perhaps imagine. But something else. Whatever it was that Charlie longed for after he had come home. She had seen it, though he had tried to disguise it, some yearning in him. The not wanting to be here, but there, wherever. The same yearning she sensed in Hussey, who seemed anxious again to be gone. She shook his hand again slow and cool in hers, seeing him off back to his blue hills and the boys bringing him tea on the veranda. He was a studious and thoughtful man, Charlie had said, if a little dry and academic, a classicist by training, an ethnographer by inclination. Surely such a man had observed, and could have told her what he and Charlie knew, which he might have explained to her, intelligently and rationally, coolly as a man does who knows Latin and Greek? If she had asked.

He was talking about the Mau Mau, wasn't he? Richard said on the way home. Richard had watched the news on television.

Jonny asked, What's maumau?

You wouldn't understand. It's politics. In Kenya, where that man came from, where he's ruling the blacks.

But what is it? You haven't said what it means.

It's the terrible things you see, that you never forget. Richard wouldn't tell him more. He would keep his advantage over his little brother.

Oh, Jonny said. I know what maumau is.

———

The winter wheat ripened. There had been rain in the spring, heavy showers in May and June, and after the rain the sun came out. The crop had grown thick and tall. This last crop would be the best Charlie had ever planted.

It was to be a fine harvest.

A fine summer.

Fine days broke, morning after morning – and she woke early those mornings, she woke early and watched the light grow and did not go back to sleep – the blue sky bright and empty, as if there was some hollowness there that set off an echo until there was such activity about her that it could no longer be heard.

That man invited us to Africa. Can we go?

Ah, you mean Mr Hussey. Did Mr Hussey tell you things?

No. He talked to Jonny though, about the things that Daddy did in the jungle.

Did he?

Or maybe Jonny made it up. Jonny's silly, isn't he?

Well, he's younger than you are. You have to let him have his stories.

So, can we go?

Who needs to go to Africa? It's so hot and sunny here.

Let them not go to Africa. Let them not know such things.

———

When the combine came out into the field in front of the house, she drew the curtains. She heard her mother's voice from the past, her house-proud mother telling her when she had first come to live here that the sun came too brightly into the south-facing room, that she must draw the curtains in the daytime lest the light fade the pictures and damage the furnishings. There weren't watercolours in the room any more, she had moved the watercolours long ago and put up other pictures instead, and had the chairs re-covered, but she kept the room dim nonetheless like the urban girl she had once been, her mother's daughter who, when she came to the house, so anxious to do things right, had once worried about things like the light bleaching the upholstery. The curtains only muffled the sound a little – for how could she keep the windows closed on a hot July day? She sat in the room with the windows open and the curtains blowing, motes of dust dancing in the light that entered between the moving curtains, and heard other men and machines gather this crop that Charlie had planted. She had to let the boys go out to watch. She couldn't keep them in. The men had said they would be good to them. She had to trust these other men, but she would not see them. Come out with us, Mum, the boys said, but she wouldn't. No, I've seen it before, lots of times, you remember how we've seen it before. When they came back at the end of the day hot and dusty and exhilarated she had made them a cake for tea. But they saw that she was sad. Jonny saw, at least. It's all right, Mummy, I won't go tomorrow, he said, I'll stay with you, and she said, Well then let's take a trip to the seaside, so long as this weather lasts, that would be nice, wouldn't it? Only Richard wanted to be with the men. They went out in the morning before the work had begun, with blankets and a picnic, and a striped windbreak because even in July the wind off the North Sea could be cold. Richard sulked all the way as they drove. When they got there he threw stones and kicked the sand into the waves, and when they swam he dared Jonny out of his depth and ducked him until he ran away up the beach crying. They came home late in the afternoon. The combine was still going, moved on to the next field. Inland the air had kept hot and dry, and the combine would keep going well into the dusk. All right, Richard, you can run out now, if the men will have you. But do ask the men first, won't you? She saw him go and felt that she had lost him. He was boy, all boy, running out in his red shorts to the roar of the machines and the cloud where the combine worked. She picked up the jumper that he had left on the kitchen chair and ran after him a little way – Take this with you, it'll get cold later – but he was too fast for her and she came back in. That boy-ness in him she could not touch.

One weekend late that same summer, she invited a male friend to stay. There had been other friends to stay, women and couples, but never before a single man. It was August, lovely weather, the harvest almost done, the dust of it still in the air. Michael was an old flame. He had even proposed to her once, before she met Charlie, and perhaps he might one day have proposed to her again. She might just possibly have come to marry him – later, not then, then would have been far too soon, only some-time much later. But none of that was in her mind at the time, only that he was a good, kind, sympathetic man, and he tried hard with the boys. He drove up on the Saturday in a convertible Sunbeam and squeezed them all in and took them out for a ride, parked it outside the front door when they came back and let the boys play in it till teatime when he put up the roof. And he had brought them presents, well chosen considering he was a bachelor, Airfix models and the latest *Beano*. Perhaps he tried too hard. The visit was a disaster.

The Sunday was hot and beautiful. They had lunch outside where the French windows from the sitting room opened onto the lawn. Michael had brought wine from London, in a green Italian bottle wrapped with raffia. It was a treat. One didn't drink wine much in those days. The two of them sat on after lunch and drank the last of the wine while the boys went off to play. They could hear the sound of a combine in the distance, on Jackson's land, not theirs, on the fields closest to the village – or she heard it, perhaps Michael had not been aware of it at all. If she had married Michael then she would have sold the farm and they would have gone to live in London, she supposed, or Tunbridge Wells, some place close to London from which he could have commuted to the City, and it would have been some quite other life, and she and the boys would have left all this behind. She liked the wine, and Michael's conversation was easy. She told him of her plans for the garden. If she had married him she would have needed a garden. So it should have been Tunbridge Wells. She told him how bare it was when she first arrived, Uncle Ralph's hybrid teas had grown out of hand, Virginia creeper swallowing the back of the house – though there were touches that were beautiful, like the lilacs Ralph had planted, the mass of daffodils long established beneath the sycamores that made the place so glorious in the spring. She told him how she had drawn plans and planted the hedges, separating her garden from the land about, and planted the roses within it. You've worked wonders, he said, and they got up from the table and walked around and she told him what else she planned to plant, suddenly immersed in the moment as she so rarely was in those days. Oh, but I'm getting carried away, you don't have a garden, do you, you can't be interested in all of this! Michael said, But of course I am, and smiled, his eyes to hers, and she realised how close they were standing and in that instant turned away. Too soon, it was far too soon. Was it love or sympathy or loneliness that hung between them, the thread that she felt between her hand and his, so close to her even as she turned? Now where can the boys have got to? she said then. She would hide behind the boys. That had become her refuge when people began to touch her: being their mother, no more, making that a barrier between herself and the rest of the world. They were here just a moment ago, she said. They were climbing the walnut tree. There was a rope hanging from the tree that they used to climb to the first branch, where they could spy on the garden unseen behind the leaves.

I saw them run off, Michael said.

When?

Now. Only just now.

Oh. Oh well, they'll come back soon enough.

Do you think we should look for them?

No. I'm sure they'll be back before you leave.

The conversation had died. She didn't know what to speak of any more. They walked to the front of the house. Perhaps the boys were playing in his car again, but they weren't. They went inside and Michael fetched down his case, and still the boys were nowhere to be seen. She must find them to say goodbye.

It's all right, you can say goodbye for me.

She called their names, up the stairs. Surely they could not be indoors, upstairs on a day like this?

Really, it's fine, there's no need to find them for me. Only I must get going. It's a long drive.

They said goodbye, just the two of them, with a look but no kiss. And he started the car, and waited a moment. She thought that the sound of the engine might have drawn the boys, but she stood alone and watched as he drove away.

She found them in the greenhouse.

Had there been an earthquake? It looked as if there had been an earthquake.

Terracotta rubble, soil, leaves beneath their feet as if a miniature terracotta city had been destroyed. The two boys giants in the ruins.

Jonny saw her first and stood transfixed, terrified, but Richard held a hoe in his two hands and went on smashing things. The pots in which tomatoes grew, the plants torn out and thrown down and the thick scent of their crushed leaves in the air, ripening fruits squashed green and red underfoot. Other pots swept down from the shelves, ten-inch pots, eight-inch pots, four-inch pots, the towers of tiny pots in which she grew seedlings, thrown down and smashed, one after another, among the sieves and seed trays. She couldn't speak. At last Richard saw her and held still, but shaking, the tool he held trembling in the air, as if arrested but not halted in his movement, hair blond, eyes blue, rooted in the chaos like a sturdy wild Vandal warrior. Everything about them seemed to hold utterly still as she took a step forward onto the debris. She felt shards crack further beneath her feet. Heard them break. As if there was a whole ruined city, a civilisation, the work of ages beneath her feet.

How could they do this?

Another step, and she saw Richard's eyes dart to the glass above their heads. Would he have raised the hoe and smashed that too? With one final blow? The sky glittering down on them, glass breaking, falling, cutting boys' skin? Glass in their eyes. No, tears. Tears in all of their eyes.

He's gone, she said. Now come in and have tea.

They left the ruins without a word.

They need a father figure, her friends had said.

But they had their figure.

There was a figure, a shadow, a voice that echoed through the spaces of the house. That caught the imaginary cricket balls they threw, or batted them back. Or missed.

Howzat?

———

That September the boys went away to school. That was what people did, in those days. It made so much sense, people said, for the two of them to go, and together. It'll be good for them, people said, they'll be just like all the other boys when they're there. People always had things to say. People tried to press you into the normal. To imitate the normal even if that wasn't what you were. They wanted you to live whatever pattern it was that they themselves lived. If you weren't a whole family then you had to live always in the lack of it.

No, it wasn't correct to say that they went. She sent them. She drove them to the school and left them there.

The hall of the school was huge. There were other mothers hugging sons goodbye. Some fathers too, but more mothers than fathers. Richard cried. Jonny didn't. It's all right, one of the other mothers said, he'll be running around and playing soon enough, soon as you're out of sight.

This she must believe, that her son would have another life once he was out of her sight. Her two sons, everyone, they all had other lives when you did not see them. Like their father had done. Some other life, out of sight.

She drove away from the school, the tall brick building with all its windows and chimneys, away down the drive and along the road, and turned off the road into a lay-by and herself cried. It was some time before she was ready for the drive home. She took a handkerchief from her handbag and dried her face. She turned the rear-view mirror so that she could see herself, tidied her make-up and put on lipstick, though there would be no one but herself to see her, tightened her lips one against the other, sighed, and drove on. It was late afternoon. The school would be feeding them tea. She imagined the mass of boys, her boys in the mass, their shorts, their long socks striped at the tops, their bare knees, their tousled hair. Somehow she could not see their faces. She drove the twenty miles home. Driving was slow in those days though there was scarcely any traffic on the road. It was almost dusk by the time she got home. A pity, she thought, because she might have done some gardening. As it was, she got home and unlocked the door, and let Jess out, Jess impatient to be out, and she walked the garden watching the dog, still holding the key that she had not thought to put down, and in the nice shoes that she had worn to go to the school though the ground was wet.

One noticed as it got dark how the yellows stood out. The yellow flowers held their colour as other colours dulled, the yellow flowers and the first yellow leaves. She always remarked on that, how in autumn as the sun grew low some colours seemed to hold its light, the last of the goldenrod and the rudbeckia and then some asters that were just coming out, a particular variety of aster that had pale mauve petals and a yellow centre that shone out in the dusk. Something to do with the spectrum, Charlie had once told her, and whatever type of ray of sunlight it was that bent over the curve of the horizon, some piece of science which she had never quite bothered to understand. What need to understand what was there before one's eyes? She walked until the last hint of colour was lost. The dog was back at the door before her.

She woke in an empty house. Did the chores of the morning downstairs, not going back up. She would have Mrs T clean the boys' room when she came on Tuesday. She would leave it till then. Until then she could not bear to enter it.

It was as if they were out with Charlie. He had come and taken them away. Hey, boys, do you want to come out with me, shoot some rabbits, there were a hundred rabbits on the Five Acre today, we need to scare them off, but come quickly while I've got time – no, don't tell your mother, she'll fuss over your coats, it's not cold, come as you are – and they'd gone out, the three of them with Jess. But Jess was home in the kitchen, on the rug in front of the Aga. Jess hadn't gone. They weren't out there on the Five Acre, the tall man and the two boys, the man and the older of the boys carrying guns and the younger one the lead to the golden dog (but only to give him something to do, because the dog was well trained and needed no lead at a time like that), and the bunnies scattering away from them. And if they hadn't been there, then they wouldn't be in the spinney either. Jess raised her head. Come on, Jess, let's go for a walk. The dog rose, and she put on her boots and this time it was she who took up the lead, not attaching it, only putting it into her pocket, just in case, since she was walking blind, did not know where they were going and whether or not they would chance to meet livestock or find themselves walking along a road where the lead would be needed, and went out. The sky was a deep blue September sky but smudged low across the landscape here and there where men were burning stubble. There was barely a wind, only the highest leaves of the trees faintly moving and a tinge of burning in the air. It felt as still outdoors as it had been in the house, where only she had moved and the dog, but in the distance she could see that the men were taking advantage of the stillness to get the burning done, setting thick bands of smoke flowing across the fields. When she got to the Five Acre it was already burnt, the ground satin black. No pickings left for the birds. Jackson must have burnt it just the day before. Always quick on the job, old Jackson, Charlie used to say. Doesn't let the grass grow under his feet – or the stubble lie. Jackson had been quick to take up a contract on the land. Charlie would have expected that, would have expected him to take over the farm and would probably have thought him the best man for the job. He's a bit of a hard man, but a good farmer, Jackson, Charlie would say, looking over at his neighbour's fields. Why was it that Charlie's voice kept coming back to her now, ringing in her ears? Well it was gone now, the last of the last crop that he had planted. She felt hard as Jackson. Tougher now that it was burnt and gone.

Flakes of black straw hung in the hedges. Her walking stirred the ground so that she had the taste of ash on her lips. The spinney was up ahead. No, not that way, Jess, not today. We'll go back the way we came.

She went back and worked all of the rest of the day in the garden. That day, and the ones that followed. Never did she work so hard in the garden as in that time after the boys went away to school. It was early for lifting and dividing and replanting, but if she did it with care the plants would not mind. Besides, it was so much easier to imagine how they would look in their new positions, next year, how the border might be rearranged, when the plants still had their leaves to them and a touch of colour, and one could see the form of the clumps. So much of gardening was that, the labour carrying one outside of the present moment and into the future, imagining how the garden would be, next year, another year, any year but this one.

She felt a shadow above her as if someone was standing there. Charlie darling, she said without looking up, yet she knew even as she spoke, but only a piece of her knew, that the shadow was not made by Charlie there but only a branch of the crabapple which she had moved beneath as she forked up weeds. So much she used to talk to Charlie about her plans for the garden.

Autumn crocuses, that's what we are missing. I wonder when it's best to plant them? In the winter, do you think, like the cyclamen? Look how well the cyclamen I planted the first year are doing, under the cherry tree, they've begun to naturalise, the clump bigger now every year. And Charlie might say, But I thought crocuses came in the spring. And she would say, with a flash of irritation, That's why these are called autumn ones, silly. I thought you knew about that sort of thing.

She had thought he knew. But he didn't know. And he had brought her here.

Then she would fall within herself. She would feel herself falling, and have to grip the fork and work the harder. In the night, too, she would feel herself falling, when she woke in the night, or in the morning when she woke so early, she would feel herself falling behind closed lids and have to pull herself up before she could open her eyes to the day.

They had worked so hard at it all, learning all they had learnt, softening it with banter, he learning to farm, she making it her job to make things light, learning at the same time whatever it was she had to do, to be a good wife to him however he was, to cook, to be a house-wife, a mother; and they had been happy, hadn't they, for a time? Was that as happy as one was supposed to be, all things considered? Surely it was, as happy as others were, as others anyway appeared to be? They were doing whatever it was they were supposed to be doing, then, at that time, and what others were doing; but it wasn't ever quite right. Normal, so normal; but they were in the wrong life. Charlie in the wrong life, trying to make the farm work, to be what such a man was supposed to be, then, at that time. She too. Had she known it even then, at the beginning? Had he? Or had it only come to him later, to make it clear to them both? To make it clear, and clear off, leave her behind. And now she was the one here, still here, doing it all still, for her boys.

———

Take the plunge, others said. You need a life of your own. They'll get used to it soon enough.

Yes, maybe.

Or maybe not.

Now and then over the next year or so, in the term time when the boys were gone, Michael came to stay.

She had Mrs T make up the spare room for him but the second time he came he slept in her bed, returned to his, sometimes but not always, before morning. What Mrs T noticed she couldn't say. It wasn't only Mrs T but the house that seemed to demand the propriety, even when almost a year had passed. Of course Michael, like most of the men she knew, had been in the war, but in the Navy, on the Arctic convoys. He almost never spoke of it. Only once he had mentioned that it was cold. And frightening? she had asked. Yes, he said, very frightening. But that was all he said, nothing else. And not a piece of it showed in him. How could she live again with a man who did not speak? Michael or any of these men she met. She was becoming used to being alone now, she knew that it wouldn't work. She knew that it could be as lonely inside a relationship as outside of one. So she let him stay, only that. Sleep with her. She never told him about the broken city. Later there would be others, but never for long.

———

At half-term and end of term, she collected the boys from school and brought them home, driving and asking them questions as she drove, glancing across or back at them in the passenger seats, impatient to close the gap that had opened when they had been away. Each time, they looked the same and yet not the same. Each time, they knew more things that she didn't know, Test Match scores, names of cars on the road, boys' knowledge that set them apart. Never before had they had lives apart from hers. Billy would be there to help lift their trunks from the car and upstairs. Billy would greet them as if they'd never been away, Jess jump up and lick their faces and skitter after them about the rooms.

The noise was so sudden, even if long anticipated, breaking the accumulated silence of weeks. Was this how it had been, she thought, before? Last time? The boys or the sound of them seemed to fill every room at once.

Then there was the smell of them, the smell on the clothes that she unpacked the next day from the trunks and took in a great heap to carry down to wash. The dirt, the mess, the dried mud on their rugger boots that fell off in the pattern of their studs onto the bedroom carpet. So much she had forgotten, each time. She should have thought to have Billy leave the trunks downstairs so that she might have put all the dirty things into the scullery straightaway.

The summer holiday was the greatest liberation of all. The boys ran wildly through the house. With wind-milling arms they mimed bowling, through the rooms and up the stairs. As she came onto the landing with their sports clothes in her arms she almost collided with Richard. She dropped all the clothes, shorts, shirts falling, as a hard red ball passed fast and close to her head and smashed the window behind her.

I didn't mean to let go, Richard said. I was only practising my action. He cupped his hand again as if it held the ball. See, this is how I learnt to do it. Slowly, with deliberation, he raised his arm, wheeled it back and up, released his fingers, with a little twist of the wrist for spin. Like that, he said, his blue eyes direct and without apology.

But that ball was real, she said. It was a hard cricket ball. It might have hurt me.

He too, she saw, was real, substantial as the ball, separate from her idea of him. He had grown while he was away, at once taller and less sturdy. She thought of him always as such a sturdy boy. It would not be long before he was as tall as she was, but he was bold as if he had that height already, looking at her boldly eye to eye.

If you have a ball, she said, then you must do your bowling outside.

Outside, there was glass on the grass. She had to put on leather gloves and pick it up, piece by piece, before any person or animal walked there. She would wrap the pieces in newspaper before she put them in the dustbin. She didn't want anyone cutting themselves. One of the splinters had made a tiny nick on her finger, where there was a tear in a glove. She took off the glove and put the cut to her mouth to suck away the blood. He was standing at the door watching.

You'll have to pay for that window. You can clear out the garage and earn some money and pay for the glass.

She couldn't help thinking how like his father he was. Those blue eyes, the squareness of the face, the long back that meant that he would be tall. Regular features, thick fair hair that wouldn't brush down. Some silent weight in him, that she had found in Charlie, that she had not seen at first, that she had got to recognise over the years of their marriage, ugly and intractable. She had observed Richard intensely from the day he was born, because he was the first, and later perhaps with a kind of foreboding because he was like his father. He said nothing, but doggedly cleared the garage. He spent the whole day doing it. Never before and never again would she see it so tidy.

A morning like others

Time passed. Times returned. All days began the same way. They always had, days at the farm, days in the country, waking in her bed to that day's degree of morning light.

This had been specifically a day in November. November one year was not so different from November any other. This particular morning there was almost no light at all, only a glimmer of grey where the curtains did not meet.

She woke, half woke, as he rose from the bed. He let in the cold between the sheets, so she pulled them closer when he was gone and curled back into herself and into sleep. Half-sleep.

What happened next she might have remembered or she might have imagined later, because the beginning of this day was indistinguishable really from that of so many other days. It was possible, after all, that this was one of the mornings when Charlie's movements didn't wake her and she slept on regardless, even spreading out into the warm space that he had left; but then there would have been no narrative, and memory requires narrative, requires this day to begin in consciousness. So there it was. In her memory she heard, half heard, him dress, open the door quietly so as not to wake her, pull it to, pad downstairs in his socks. She would think that he was wearing burgundy-coloured socks, because he had only one pair that colour, and it occurred to her later, when she cleared all his clothes, that she never saw them again. (The small things and the worn things taken from his drawers, folded as they were, and burned in the incinerator which was a black barrel at the back of the yard; other things given away; those particular socks never seen.)

He padded down the stairs, dark red foot after dark red foot, past the sporting prints dim on the wall, to the kitchen. (Uncle Ralph's prints still there, before she redecorated and took them down.) Or first to his study, perhaps, to the gun cupboard there. Either then or later he took out the Purdey and a handful of cartridges to put in the pocket of his coat – or perhaps the cartridges were already in his pocket, for there would have been no reason for him to take so many if his intention were clear. Often she had found cartridges left in the pocket of his coat, even working their way through tears into the lining, weighing it down when you lifted it though the pockets when you turned them out were empty. The coat was of thick greenish Harris tweed, heavily worn. (That did not come back to her. If it had, then she might have kept it and put her hands to the tough weave and taken in its smell which had seemed to her so essentially a smell of him.)

Did she hear the shot? Her memory told her that she did. But this was a morning like many others. There had been other mornings when there were shots, when he or Billy had gone out early. One shot was much like another, coming from some indeterminate direction dully across the fields. The death of a rabbit sounds much the same as the death of a man. If she heard the shot she thought nothing of it, but only dozed the longer because it was a Saturday morning and there was no need to wake the boys to take them to school. Thank goodness for that, she thought, when finally she got out of bed and walked yawning across the room to draw the curtains, thank goodness, because there was such thick fog outside. They were still at the village school then; that was then, before, when they all lived at home and she drove them each day the mile to school. There was nothing she hated more than driving the boys to school in winter fog, leaning forward to the windscreen as if that would help her to see better, wiping the condensation with the back of her hand, worrying that there might be ice, at the same time going over their spelling or their tables with them as advancing bands of fog seemed to materialise in the headlights. No school this morning, but there would be homework, for Richard at least; not for Jonny as he was too young. She thought as she got up that she would make them all a good breakfast. Charlie would like that, if he had already been outside in the cold. But what could he be doing outside, in this fog? Not shooting, surely? And yet hadn't there been a shot? He would barely be able to see further than the end of his nose. (And was it then at the time or was it only later when she remembered, that this simple thoughtless thought turned cold in her? How could she think that, why think that, just then? The day just passed, the day before, the evening just passed, had been a slow, easy day, an easy evening. Perhaps even for some days before it had been so, she could not count them now. Only she knew that there had been some time of calm, before. The brooding that was sometimes such a weight in him had seemed to be gone, that previous evening at least, like mud gone from his boots. How could that be, she would think later. Surely there had been a sign, something in his behaviour, some premonition? What had she seen, and what missed? Possibly the calm itself was the sign, a calm that meant that his plan was made and the intention had given him ease. And she had lived with him through those days and slept beside him through the nights, and known nothing. If these questions were not with her at the time then they would be with her ever after.)

He had made himself a black coffee before he went out. That was all. There was only the cup on the table with the dregs of the coffee. She thought, when she came down, how he would be needing a good breakfast when he came in.

He had stoked the Aga. The oven was good and hot.

It was kind of him to do that, she would think later. If he had in his mind what he was about to do, then it was a kind thought – or was it only thoughtless habit, persisting regardless, the habit of their lives, or proof that he meant to come back, after all, or just an option left open? He had taken the time on this his last morning to stoke up the stove so that his family should be warm when they came downstairs, and the bacon when she cooked it, if he were to come to eat it, would be crisp. (But he can't have been thinking of them, not then. He can't have been thinking of anyone but himself. It was so selfish, what he was doing, so appallingly, abominably selfish.)

What then? What happened next?

Calling to the boys upstairs. Hearing them moving, coming down.

The knock at the back door. Billy, the constable, the bedraggled dog held by a string tied to her collar, some other men.

I had to be putting her on the string, madam. She wouldn't be going otherwise. I'd call her and she'd come along a little ways, and then she'd run back.

Thank you, Billy, she had said, taking the string in her hand, bending to untie it from the dog's collar.

The men came on in, crowding the kitchen. Men who looked useless, their hair damp, eyes looking about, evasive; the smell of them the smell of a wood in the morning mixed with tobacco smoke. She wondered why they were all of them there; if the dog had been found straying somewhere, why they had all of them taken it upon themselves to bring the dog home? They looked about, shuffled. The boys had come in at the same time.

Perhaps we should go into another room, Mrs Ashe.

Yes, the sitting room. Just herself and the constable and Billy now. Billy had barely ever been in the sitting room before though he came almost daily to the kitchen. They didn't sit in the room but only stood. That annoyed her. She felt annoyed with them for making her go there, for coming to her and taking her there to say whatever it was they were going to say, which already perhaps she knew, which was why she was angry. They were so awkward, standing there before her. Better if they had gone back outside. Outside at least they would have had space around them for what needed to be said. No weight of ceiling over their heads. No things pressing about them, no soft carpet or curtain or upholstery, but only cold space.

I have to go out and see. I want to see.

Are you sure? Perhaps you should wait a while, madam, let us bring him in first.

Yes. No. Now.

She led them back into the kitchen, where just the boys and the dog now remained, and spoke to Billy, her eyes to his high above the boys' eyes, adult to adult. Her voice surprisingly controlled. Billy, would you be very kind and stay with the boys just a bit?

She put on her coat, hastily tied a scarf over her head.

Took up her gloves from where they lay on the table.

Put on her boots by the back door. Jonny's stood beside them, neatly placed but wet with mud. How odd, could he have been out already? The thought registered but only superficially. It was nothing beside the shock of the other thoughts in her.

The air was cold, moist with fog.

The constable spoke plain words to prepare her. It's a bit of a mess, Mrs Ashe. Might be best if you could wait and see him later, when they've tidied him up a bit.

How could she say that she must see the place? See him. Be outside in the cold air where words were not only words but visible as breath?

The constable knelt on the leaves on the ground of the spinney and lifted the edge of the coat that had been thrown over him. That was enough. She did not need to see the rest. She saw the twisted way that he lay, the length of his body, his hand that had let go its hold on the gun. The constable looked up at her with a question and she managed the smallest shake of the head that stopped him from going any further, an answer in her eyes as much as anywhere. No more.

In the kitchen, the boys had got themselves some cereal.

Billy had made a pot of tea. Always until now it had been she who made tea for Billy. He had made the strong tea she kept especially for him. Thought you'd be needing it, Billy said, his hands shaking as he poured her a cup, unsure of themselves, slopping milk white onto the blue-and-white saucer. Such competent hands they had seemed to her until now, big rough knobbly countryman's hands, reddened with work or with cold.

The boys sat in their chairs and watched.

There's been an accident, she said. She heard herself say that as if it was someone else's voice speaking. She didn't know what to say next.

She remembered the bacon then, that she had put in the oven before. She grabbed the oven glove, knelt before the stove, opened the door onto smoke.

The rashers quite black, welded to the roasting tray.

The tray hot through the glove.

She dropped the tray into the sink and ran water onto it. Stood back from the steam escaping the white walls of the sink.

The boys were watching. Billy was watching.

Think I should be off now, Billy said. If that's what you'd like, madam.

Yes, Billy. Thank you, Billy.

Boys, come to the sitting room.

Again, to the sitting room. Out of the steam and the smell of burning.

We'll be quiet there. Let's go into the sitting room. There's something I need to tell you.

Richard went stiff as ice before he cried. She saw the tears rushing to freeze in his eyes. And then he went red and they melted. But Jonny showed nothing. At first she looked at his blank face and wondered if he understood. He was just seven. What did a seven-year-old understand of death? (Everything, perhaps, or nothing. Perhaps no less than a grown woman understood. He'd seen dead things after all, birds, rabbits, rats. He knew what dead things were. Simply that when a person was dead he just *wasn't* any more.)

The dog had come into the room with them, crowding against their legs where they sat all three on the sofa. She had her arms around the boys and then she held the dog. She felt the dog's warmth, and the slight shiveriness within her, smelled the world outside that she had brought to them inside. She sensed that the dog understood. The dog of course had been there.

Daddy's had an accident, she said. That voice again, that might not have been hers. She said that he tripped when he was climbing a fence and the gun went off. It seemed a plain enough story for boys to understand, even if boys knew that a man shouldn't be climbing a fence with a loaded gun. But clearer because of that, because they would assume that if a man were to do such a thing, and the gun were indeed to go off, then he might well die as a consequence. It was the sort of thing one said, wasn't it? At the time, in her world, among people like herself – themselves.

Only much later did she think about the mud on Jonny's boots. It was too late by then. Her lie was told, fixed from that first moment as fact. It wasn't the sort of lie one could go back on. If he had been outside that morning, if he had followed his father, if he had seen what might have been seen outside, then one could only hope that he hadn't noticed that what she said was different from what was there; he was only seven, after all. It wasn't meant as a lie, but as a way to make truth gentle. An accident, she had said it was, with the two boys beside her on the sofa, and the dog, who knew but didn't know her words, before them. And Jonny was closed in on himself, but so was his brother with the tears like ice in his eyes; the two boys, each so different, each closed away. And she would be closed too, only the dog shivery but warm between them. But did they really understand? And the dog? Did Jess know he was gone for ever or was she looking for him each time that she went to the door and whimpered? Jess attached herself most to Jonny after that, though it made Richard jealous. Every day Jonny took her for a walk when he came back from school. If it was raining and Claire said he couldn't go, he was angry with her.

But, Mummy, Jess has to have her walk. She hates to be in the house all day.

I've already taken her. We walked to the village this morning. All right then, you can go out for a short walk, when the rain stops. She's an old dog now, she doesn't need to go too far.

It helped to take the dog with her when she went to the village. The dog was a shield against the kindness of the people who stopped to talk. A golden place for them to put awkward and pitying hands.

Cricket

The Green, they called it, the place where they played. That was what it was, green. Men in white stood in a pattern on the green. She was a Japanese girl in a picture postcard of England, sitting on a striped deckchair watching cricket. Wearing sunglasses. Sipping lemonade through a straw.

Claire sat in a chair beside her. Now and then one of her friends came and sat with them. Jonathan had been lying on the grass until a short time before but he had gone to prepare to bat. His trousers were too big. They were Richard's. He looked comical in the baggy trousers that now had green stains on them from the grass. His team had been batting for a long time. He was one of the last to go in. She could see that he was afraid that he would do badly. He had not played cricket since he left school. It was Richard's game, he said, not his, it had always been Richard's game. Richard was good, even Kumiko could see that. He looked good playing. He looked tall and strong in the white clothes and his hair was bright in the sun. He stood very still as the bowler ran in, and then he raised the bat and hit the ball a long way. He went out to bat at the beginning of the match, second or third, and he was still there. Claire had explained the rules to her, but she didn't think you needed to know the rules to watch. She didn't mind about the rules. She watched the men moving across the Green, and the little clouds, and the swallows flying over. And the other people watching, children running about, mothers calling them back.

No one would have guessed they were brothers, seeing them there, Richard looking so heroic, Jonathan dark and tense and restless, fidgeting with his bat while the bowler got ready, tapping the grass with it as if that would make a difference. Then looking up, facing the ball, hitting it away just a short distance so that he scored a run and went to the other end and Richard could take his place.

He looked exposed there out on the grass. Yet he had as much reason to belong as all the other villagers. He had been born in this village. He had lived in it for at least twenty of his twenty-five years. He seemed apart, even here where he came from, standing with his bat, looking about him, ready again to run as soon as his brother hit the ball.

Do you know, Claire said, sometimes when he was away he didn't write home for months. We had no idea where in the world he was.

She said, I think he was on the move a lot, travelling. Maybe some letters did not get to you.

She could understand why he didn't mention it when he went to Vietnam. He would have known how much that would have worried her. She let the words drop and didn't speak them. Easy to do that, as the bowler bowled and Richard tapped the ball away, and the bowler bowled again, and Richard hit hard and clean, Jonathan running forward a couple of steps and then relaxing as the ball flew out across the grass to where the spectators were on the other side of the ground. It was careless of him, Kumiko thought, not to write. For Claire, here in the permanence of their home, it must have seemed that he had disappeared from the face of the earth.

As all the white figures moved around and settled again, Claire said something else. She said that his father had been missing for a long time in Asia, in the war, in the Second World War. I wasn't married to him then, she said, only engaged, and there was no word for a long time. I don't know if Jonny ever told you. No, I don't imagine that he did.

No, Kumiko said, he didn't tell me that.

All the more careless then.

The cricketers played on.

He sat on the bench in front of the pavilion, put down his batsman's gloves and then stretched out his legs, one after the other, to remove his pads.

These things he had not done in years: fastening and unfastening the worn leather straps of cricket pads, holding a bat in his hands with that scent of oil on wood, facing a ball, playing opposite his brother, knowing that there were some things that his brother had always done better. Watching his brother show off.

Was Richard always man of the match? He saw his brother walk in the midst of a group of men in white towards the pavilion entrance, throwing back his head to laugh. The women clapping, his Japanese girlfriend and his mother in colourful dresses and sunglasses like pretty ladies in the South of France.

Now I know why they made you captain, he said to Richard as he passed, and Richard waved his bat towards him as if to fend off some irony that he expected to follow.

You did OK yourself. Richard was unusually complimentary, not winding him up like he used to do in the past; perhaps things had changed just so much.

I survived. Don't say any more. Didn't let you down anyway.

This was coming home. To old patterns. Old selves that he hadn't known for a while but just about fitted, like the clothes in his cupboard. A summertime self, the mediocre batsman whose purpose was simply to be safe and not to be out. There was almost a comfort in it, finding that this old self fitted and that the others fitted around him.

———

He crept down the passage to her bed, the whole length of the house, from his room to hers. I heard you coming, she whispered. He thought he had been as quiet as ever but she had been listening for him.

You played well, at the cricket, she said.

Kind of you to say that, but it's not entirely true.

Well, Richard was better.

Richard's always better.

There was a sound at the window. For a moment she froze.

What's the matter?

There's something at the window. Like someone scratching against the glass.

They listened.

Oh, I know what it is, she said. It's only a rose. It's Madame Alfred Carrière. She must have come loose again. Your mother told me her name.

Afterwards they lay with the sheet away to the side of them.

You never told me about your father, she said. What happened in the war.

His hand was in her hair. She loved to feel his hand in her hair.

I said he was in the Burma campaign.

You didn't say that he was missing. That everyone must have thought he was dead.

Oh, didn't I?

And then he said, Does it matter?

I don't know, she said. I think it does.

He pulled up the sheet then and wrapped himself around her but they didn't sleep for a while. There was the white rose scratching at the glass of the open window, and beyond it, the night. The night lay over the house and all the fields and the woods, and there were sounds in it. The sounds were strange to her. A lone raw cry, eerie, came from somewhere beyond the garden, towards the wood.

What was that? Was it something being killed?

It's a fox.

A fox killing something? It sounds like the cry of whatever the fox killed.

Just a fox being a fox, I think.

Calling its mate?

Mating.

Can't foxes mate silently?

His laugh ran through them like a tremor.

Next time we come, I'll tell Mum we'll both sleep here in the spare room.

Yes, she said. Yes, that will be much better.

We'll still be quiet.

Of course.

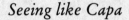

Seeing like Capa

In Tokyo there had been no need to carry his past with him but only his camera. When people asked, What are you, Who are you, he might say no more than his name, that he was English and a photographer, or an English teacher when he didn't feel like saying that or the photography didn't pay. There was a whole community of English teachers. Some of them weren't even English but that didn't matter because the Japanese who were their students generally couldn't tell the difference. They were a travelling flotsam with identities that might or might not be true, with grand or less grand notions of themselves and stories they told or stories they didn't tell. And if you liked to take pictures, you could do what you liked and take pictures of anything anywhere. Because you were gaijin, and nothing was expected of you.

You off on the hippy trail? his brother had said, before he went travelling. That was what some of their friends were suddenly doing, taking off in buses or camper vans, overland to India, coming back with long hair and chillums and ill-cured Afghan coats.

No. Not exactly.

That was when he first put a word to what he meant to be. A photographer. Though he didn't say it to Richard but only to himself.

He remembered what it had meant when got his first camera. It was on his twelfth birthday. He had been asking for one all year. His birthday was in June, just before the end of the summer term, and all of the holiday that followed he took the camera about with him, photographing everything in sight. That was when it started. He took pictures of his mother, but she got cross when he took the pictures as she hated being photographed when she wasn't prepared, so he took some of Richard, and dozens of Billy. Billy was great for pictures. Billy at work, with a spade or a barrow, with his cap and his whiskers and his old lined face looking like a country-man from any past time since photography was invented. It was great that he had the pictures, because Billy died that next winter. The best he took that September just before they were due to go back to school. He went with Billy and Richard when they went shooting. He took his camera along instead of a gun, photographed the two of them as they walked and aimed and shot, photographed the dog waiting, the dead pheasants close up with their red-rimmed eyes and fabulous feathers.

Richard liked those pictures but all the same he thought it was only a hobby. Like cricket, or shooting. It wasn't something to do with your life.

Richard had begun to take the farm in hand the year he went to university. He worked with him over that first summer's harvest, but he didn't go back to university at the end of it. He took the money Richard paid him and bought the newest Pentax. He knew what to buy. He knew something about photography by then.

Great camera, Richard said. What did it cost you?

It cost him a lot. His travelling would have to be cheap because he had spent so much on the camera. He would have to earn along the way. The camera had to be a good one because it was to be his eye on the world. It would be the means to give what he saw physical presence. The evidence of his seeing – or of his being, if you followed the thought through. That, his grand notion. He was going to go travelling and take pictures. He would be what he did and not what he was. What he did would make him who he was or who he would become. He would become whoever he was at any moment, with a pack on his back and a camera around his neck. Seeing the world, whatever he saw. Would he then be what he saw? Or would he always be what he had seen? (Or when he came home would he be just the same?)

Richard wouldn't get it, what he planned to do. A photographer, what sort of job was that? As if he didn't know. It was being something, someone, other than who he had been until now. Richard wouldn't know anything about that either. Richard had only ever wanted to be Richard, so far as anyone could tell.

———

When he first came back to England in December, he had laid out all of his pictures, a shiny mass of photos on the dining-room table. It looked like Pelmanism, all those memories laid out on the table to be sorted and grouped together, in the dining room where they had once played cards, the cards face down across the tablecloth.

Richard came in to see. Richard was never so good at cards. It was the one game that Jonny could win despite being the youngest, as soon as he could read the numbers. He could look at the table all spread with the blue-and-red-backed playing cards and know where the matching ace was, and the eights and the twos and the kings, pick them up in a run as the game went on and the pairs revealed themselves, tight with the excitement of knowing, watching his mother's hand hovering close to the card he knew but then diving elsewhere and picking up wrong – or sometimes he suspected that that was only a ploy, that really she knew and it was only a ploy to allow him to win, once in a while, at something – then watching with glee when it was Richard's turn and Richard's hand moved blind, wrong and wrong again and right only by chance, because cards just wasn't his sort of thing.

Now Richard picked up a black-and-white print of a street cramped between high-rise buildings, vertical shop signs bearing Chinese characters. Richard was sifting through his three years. Richard himself three years older.

That Japan?

Hong Kong.

One from the next pile. A wider street, figures made nondescript by rain, umbrellas above their heads.

That's Tokyo.

Not my scene, Richard said, putting them down and looking further, restless, at one pile then another, flicking through the prints, the contact prints, the sleeves of negatives. Nothing for him there; not his turn now.

You took an awful lot of pictures.

Some of them aren't worth keeping.

Pelmanism. What matched with what? Shuffle the memories, see what matches with what, what begins, what follows. Go back to the beginning.

It had been strange to see it all here, out of the envelopes, here in the red-papered dining room with the carriage clock ticking on the sideboard and the dull Norfolk winter outside. An American called Jim who was his friend in Tokyo. Jim with two girls in the forest. One of the girls recurring in picture after picture, in the park, by the river, on the shore.

Who's the girl?

He held up a print of the girl smiling beneath a red umbrella; fine drops of rain on the lens.

That's Kumiko.

Pretty girl. Are Japanese girls pretty?

Not all of them.

She looks nice.

She *is* nice.

Putting out his hand to take the picture back. Maybe she'll come here sometime, then you and Mum can meet her.

When Richard looked up from all those photos and asked where were the others, for a moment Jonathan stalled. Which others? Oh, you mean the ones from Vietnam. But those are ages old, I've moved on from that now. I boxed them up ages ago and there's no need to look at them again. It's only the more recent ones I'm going through now – but anyway, you've seen them already. They were published, you saw that.

They were good.

They were an accident, he said, and he thought, no, in truth, they weren't good, whatever they were, in fact were a kind of failure, that brought him all the way back to where he was now, come back here to spread out these last few years on the table. And not the full years, edited years at that.

No, surely not, Richard was saying. Not an accident, not at the time?

It was all a crazy thing, he said, some of the cool of those days coming back to him, being cool again as if he still had the camera slung about his neck, light meter dangling, though he was here at home in the dining room and with only his brother to see — and you never quite grew up at home, you were never so free as elsewhere, always aware, wary, of what had gone before, what might pull you back, always the danger there that your big brother would see through you to someone smaller.

That's how it was out there, he said, trying now to be accurate. Truthful, not tough.

I was just travelling, and I met someone who was going to the war and he said it was easy, easy to get there, easy to go, and it was, and there it was before me. I was only in the country for a few weeks. I just struck it lucky, that's all.

People who stayed home, people like Richard, didn't understand how easy travel was. Even to a place like that. Because everything was immediate, every decision and move made for the moment, for that day. Eat, travel, find a place to sleep. Move on. A day at a time. Or maybe consider just the day after or the day after that.

Those pictures were great. Aren't you going to do more like that?

That war's over now.

There are other wars.

No.

People, people all over, wanted to see what he had seen. They looked, and they might remember those images he had taken through all the rest of their lives, in place of other images, even in place of first-hand ones that might have made them happy. He had told himself there was meaning in it. Purpose. And then the cheque came in, and he moved to Tokyo where there was no war, and bought a leather jacket, and packed away the prints and the negatives into their boxes. He took them out once to show Kumiko and afterwards regretted it.

No, I'm not going to do that again, he said. Too much maumau.

'Maumau' shut Richard up. 'Maumau' was a word they had between them, just in the family, one of those words that holds a family together and closes it against the world. 'Maumau', crushed roadkill. 'Maumau', the entrails of a poached deer thrown into a ditch. Billy knowing the sight, explaining how a deer when it was shot must be disembowelled on the spot or its meat went bad. 'Maumau', a sheep's skull he found once when they went on a walk, or Jess found it, snuffling in the bushes. He didn't know what had happened to the rest of the sheep, there was only this skull, half of it bared to the bone but the other half with dry skin still clinging to it tight and leathery, and the eye gaping through. His mother's distaste. You're not carrying that home, are you? Yes. Well you can't bring it in, it'll have maggots in it, you'll have to put it on the bonfire or bury it or something. He persisted, holding it by the bare jaw all the way back. It was interesting, weird. He thought he might do a drawing of it, strip off the rest of the skin maybe, or preserve it in something. What was it people used, formaldehyde? Do we have any formaldehyde, Mum? No, I told you, you're not bringing that smelly

94

thing in here. Take it away, it's maumau, I'm not having it in the house. The word was shorthand. Once it was said nothing more needed to be said. Though of course the thoughts would remain, the unsaid images that couldn't be forgotten. Richard knew that as well as he did. So now Richard shrugged and turned away from the photos. He went to the window, put his big hands to the frame and stared out through the glass. They both stared out. The garden was bare. Only the black hedge to see there, the stripped trees, the dead stalks of plants and the leaves on the lawn that hadn't been cleared away.

I don't think it was as easy as you say. You really worked at getting there, didn't you?

Perhaps.

Why did you go?

I don't know. Adventure. A challenge. Robert Capa.

Who's he?

A famous war photographer. He was one of the greats. He was in Spain. He was at the Normandy invasion. He went everywhere and saw everything. He was in Vietnam too, but it was still French Indochina then and it was the French they were fighting. He got killed there, sometime in the '50s.

Richard wasn't interested in anything he had to say about Capa.

I think you went because of Dad.

I don't know. Maybe in some way I did.

But you didn't see Dad's war. You saw another war.

You're right. There are lots of wars.

It was the closest moment they'd had since he had got home. Too close, in that room, on a day like that one, with the trees bare and the leaves on the ground, when the past pressed them closer. Richard took down his hands and looked at Jonny for a moment. They were men now, not boys, two men looking into each other across a room. He did not know if his brother had done that before, seen him as a man, as much a man as their father or himself. And then Richard walked out of the room and there were only the photos on the table, the pretty ones, the Japanese ones, the ones of the pretty girl, and beside all that maumau they seemed like nothing.

It was true, what he had said. It had been surprisingly easy to get in, whoever you were, that first mad modern war where photographers got to go everywhere. The trip to Vietnam had been an accident, as far as he was concerned, an aberration, as it seemed now, though at the time it had seemed intentional, fated even, the turning of a circle. Even if to others it seemed an achievement. How could he explain that to his brother? That those photos, which so impressed people that they remembered him for them, which had made a magazine cover, and which might even have been the start of a career, seemed all a mistake and even a shame. That there was no courage in them but only chance, and rush, and fear. The weight of the camera in his hands, the cold consciousness of the camera, as if only the lens saw what he himself could not bear to see and the hands were helpless to help.

Surprising how doors opened to you sometimes. Offered you a chance to be Capa, running into battle with a camera around your neck. To be a hero like Capa. Like your own father even. To see war. Shouldn't a young man see war? Wasn't the greatest photographer the photographer of war, of life and death?

Hey, Richard, see this. This is more than anything you're ever likely to see. See what your father might have seen. Get in closer. That was what Capa said made a photographer great, getting in close.

Turn war into images. Make money out of it. Let the men and women in your pictures stand for men and women anywhere. The victims, and the soldiers. Fix them in that moment in their lives or their deaths. So what if they are individuals each with their own future, who might be recognised later, those who survive, when they're not soldiers or victims any more. You don't have responsibility for them. You're only the one behind the camera. You are producing the images for other people to see, that either they think they want to see or you think they ought to see. Richard wouldn't understand how it felt. In Tokyo there had been a friend who might have understood, but he didn't see him any more. His friend had been at the war but he had been a soldier, in front of the camera, not behind it. He, like their father, like those victims, wasn't ever going to escape having been there. Even if he had a home like this to escape to, a safe home where nobody knew any of that. Where there was a view open in all directions. A wide sky. Nice clouds. Hedged fields. A girlfriend who would travel halfway across the world to visit him.

She stood at the front door.

He said, I want a picture of you there. Just like that, standing there with your back to it, like it's your house. Like a child's picture of a house and its owner.

But if I owned it, she said, I'd be going in, wouldn't I? I wouldn't be standing here looking out.

OK then, open the door and stand in the doorway.

Why?

I'm so happy to have you here, I want it to look like you belong. He was walking away with the camera, then stopping to look through the lens.

I don't belong, she said. I'm spare. I sleep in the spare room, remember?

She turned about and reached for the brass knocker. It was a big black door, with a fanlight above it. He would have a picture of the door and the back of a short Japanese girl knocking.

Take that one.

He was happy that she had come during this spell of fine weather. The garden was full of flowers. The house had the windows thrown open. This was the home that he wanted her to see. Stand at the door, I want to take a picture of you there. He had a sudden thought that he should have used black-and-white film. Somewhere in the family albums there was a picture of his mother in the same spot, a grey image of a young woman in a summer dress with one hand to the half-open door, looking out as if she was saying goodbye to someone in a departing car, of which you saw just a bulbous 1950s wing, a wheel hub and a door, and at the same time she was putting out a hand to the dog, their old retriever Jess, to stop her from running out in front of the car. But Kumiko turned to face the door and knocked. That's lovely, he said. Better that it was colour, because her yellow dress showed up so bright against the shiny black door. There was no telling what colour his mother's dress had been.

They walked through the garden, taking more pictures. Her dress became garish beside his mother's old-fashioned flowers. It was disconcerting to have her here, this girl whom he had photographed so many times, changing the perspectives in every direction, this girl who was the same girl as in all those other pictures from the year before, brought into this present which was also his past. She pushed her long black hair back behind her shoulder which was bare save for the strap of the dress and smiled her big smile. He did not know why he was taking so many pictures when she had just arrived. As if each of these moments must be recorded. When what was there came here. The shock of putting two pieces of his life together.

I did not expect, she had said, this house to be so big. Yet he thought that he had told her that before she came. The farmhouse was big and rambling. He had described all of that, and he had described the village, and the Hall where his family had once lived, which was rather more grand.

The day she arrived they had gone for a walk around the village after lunch, he and his mother and Kumiko, not Richard who was out on the farm. The three of them had walked the half-mile to the village through the fields, entering the churchyard through a gate at the back where the gravestones stood nameless, head-high in grass. Are your family here? she asked. Yes, he said, but he would not show her the graves now, not with his mother here and when she had just arrived. He showed her instead the memorials inside the church, that went back five or six centuries; an opulent slab of Victorian marble commemorating his great-grandparents who had first come to the Hall; more austere twentieth-century memorials listing villagers who had died in two world wars.

The church was tall and white, bright with the day, and silent. She walked down the aisle to the altar rail, her steps crisp on the stone floor.

May I clap, she said, or is it too quiet? Would you mind?

Go ahead.

She stood in the pool of light that fell through the east window and clapped her hands together, twice, into the white space. That's what we do when we enter a shrine, she spoke across the church to Claire. To wake the god.

So fresh and free she looked, in the yellow dress. Sunlight to blaze away the shadows. Snap.

———

Stay as long as you like, Claire said. It's lovely to have you here. It was lovely to be there, she said. She said how beautiful the place was, the house, and the garden that Claire had made, the church, the village, the way of life. Jonathan did not tell me, she said, that he grew up in such a beautiful place. She stayed the weekend and then through the following week, and then the weekend after. Jonathan had planned for them to go to London and do some sightseeing, they had even talked about going to Paris, but the summer weather continued so perfect, day after day, that it seemed a pity to leave. So they took Claire's car and went for day trips to the seaside or across the county.

They went to Swaffham on market day. To Norwich to see the cathedral. To Castle Acre and Castle Rising, those names she would remember, and to other places whose names she would forget. One day they drove past the walls of Sandringham where Jonathan said that the Queen spent her summer holiday but he didn't know if she was in residence or not. I think they have a flag flying if she's there, he said. But they did not see any flag. They did not see the house even, only those long walls and trees behind them. Maybe it was just at Buckingham Palace, he said, that she flew the flag to show when she was in. Or maybe she was not there at all, now he thought about it, he thought now it must be Christmas that she spent in Norfolk, or Easter. She had a place in Scotland for the summer.

———

One day that promised to be particularly fine, they went to the beach and he took pictures of her in the English dunes as he had taken pictures of her on a beach in Japan a year before. They went for a long walk out through the marshes and to the dunes and then on, making their way across mud and clumps of marsh grass and wet sand to a piece of land that became an island when the tide rose, and at the point at the tip of the island they saw seals playing in the sea. Then they put down their things and changed, and swam in the sea themselves. She wore the same red swimming costume as the year before, but there was a sting of wind and the sea was cold, despite the sunshine. It was a few degrees cooler on the coast than it had been inland, with that breeze and a hint of cloud coming in over the sea. This beach on the side of the island that faced the sea was long and the colouring cool, the sand pale and the beach grasses a bleached green. They ate the picnic they had brought with them and then he took pictures of her with the long pale strip of sand stretching out behind her and the endless sea horizon. No shadows, as the thin cloud moved in across the sky. The wind just so gently blowing her hair and blowing sand against her. She wrapped herself in a towel. It's cold, your English seaside. They moved back into the shelter of the dunes.

They stayed while the other trippers began to walk back.

Can't we stay here, just the two of us, she said, and play like the seals? This is so much nicer than your spare room.

But look at the time.

It won't get dark for hours.

It's not the time that matters, it's the tide. If the tide comes up we'll be cut off.

We'll have to swim.

With the picnic things?

But we have it all to ourselves now, we can play for a while.

So they did, until they saw how far the sea had come in.

They had to run for it, in their swimming things and carrying their stuff, he with his camera held high, she with the picnic basket over her head, wading through the incoming water that seemed to come so much faster once it had rounded the tips of the island. Then putting on their clothes with the wet swimming things beneath, and back across the marsh, dishevelled, wet, sandy, muddy, laughing. Driving like that home to the farm, Kumiko's black hair salt-dry and grainy with sand. Loving her like that. Not wanting to show her like that to his mother, his brother, somehow indecent as if it showed on her, the sex they had had in the dunes. But only his mother to see them when they got in, Richard not back yet.

Is there time, he said, for a bath before supper?

Yes, if you're quick.

Kumiko bathed and washed her hair, and they had supper outside because inland there was no wind and the evening was warm.

Did you have a good day? Richard asked.

Yes, he said. A very good day.

He looked across the table at her in the dusk and wanted her as much as at any time in that day. He saw her talking in that open way she had to his brother, his mother. And wondered at her, that he had brought her here or that she had come all this way for him. It was getting too dark to see the look in her eyes but he knew the heavy fall of her hair and the delicate movements of her hands. He knew all her surfaces. He had touched them and he had photographed them a thousand times. Yet here she was, foreign in his home, present and yet somehow escaping him. Here with his family about him, even at the end of this particular day, he felt that he knew her less than before. He was less sure of her, distracted by the others, by their awareness of her, by her foreignness that he noticed all at once again now as he had previously ceased to see it. He wanted to take out his camera and catch her, only the light right now was too dim for that, she sitting facing out into the garden with the light from the house, all the artificial light that there was, behind her, the light from the windows that spilled out across the lawn. It was an obsession, perhaps, photographing her. The more photographs he took, the more he realised that he would never catch her. Even though she seemed so immediate. He would catch only her stilled surface between one moment and another, never her moving self. Like those painters who paint endlessly portraits of their wives. It might be that their wives were the only people with the patience to sit for them for so long and so often, or it might be that they were trying, really trying, to capture them. Because people need to catch hold of those that they love, because even when they're very close and have been with them for a long time they can be strangers too. Only their surfaces have ever been captured, what can be painted or photographed, and their words perhaps, that can be written and recorded. Not who they are.

Was that what he was doing, taking these pictures, pictures that had no purpose, so many more hundreds of pictures than he would ever print? Fixing no more than instants, holding them in time. Now here she sat in the dusk, in light too dim for any photograph, escaping him.

What are you doing tomorrow? Richard was asking. Richard sat on the same side of the table as he did, with the window light falling clear on his face.

I don't know yet, she was saying from the shadow. Jonathan, do we have a plan for tomorrow?

Before he could think to answer, Richard said, Then you must let me show you round the farm. You haven't done that yet.

Oh yes, she said, I'd like that. Her answer came quickly. He could hear her brightness if he could not see it.

And his mother was passing the salad bowl around. Do you think it's got too dark to finish the meal out here? We could go inside for pudding. Though it's such a lovely night.

They agreed they would stay outside. A warm night such as this was rare. The moon had risen. Bats flecked the air above their heads. If no image, then a memory at least to fix. Talking across the table, darkness between them. Making the spaces that were there, the secrets and absences that their words crossed, almost tangible.

———

She went out with Richard next morning. It seemed to him that they were gone for a long time.

What took you so long?

It's a big farm, she said when she came back. I didn't know it was so big. I thought that we would walk but

Richard drove everywhere in the Land Rover. He says farmers don't walk their land, they always drive.

Well, yes, that's Richard for you. Let's go for a walk ourselves this afternoon. We're not farmers so we can walk.

The weather got muggy after lunch, the sky overcast. It wasn't a great time for a walk. Only the dog was eager to be out. He was getting attached to this new dog. Perhaps she was silly like people said spaniels were, but that might have been only her youth. She was pretty much trained but he took a lead with him because she didn't know him so well. When finally they left the house they walked out with no clear direction, down the drive and onto the track and then around the edges of the fields. He meant to take a long walk out and beyond the farm and back through the village, perhaps have a drink in the pub before they got home; they were so late that it might be open by the time they got there. They would be able to sit outside on the bench with the dog at their feet. Yet the walk seemed dull. On such a flat day the land seemed flatter than ever, the distances longer. I suppose you came all through here this morning, he said, and she said yes, she had, though of course everything looked different when you were driving.

So you know what crops he's growing.

I can tell the difference now between wheat and barley.

Barley's more beautiful, I always think. He didn't think that Richard would see a thing like that – or would he? Perhaps he would, perhaps Richard saw beauty where he did.

Richard says he wants it to rain.

Oh does he?

He says the fields could do with a little more rain before harvest.

It had become very muggy. A drop of rain fell cool on his face.

I felt rain, she said. Did you feel rain? Richard will be happy that his rain is coming.

He looked at the sky. I'm not so sure, I think this might pass. I think it might not rain at all.

The sky out there, seen from the fields, was so open and wide. Wide horizons in every direction. Cloud all across but high, he thought, too high for rain.

They were walking in the fields. She thought that it was about to rain. Jonathan was moody. He was moody at home in a way that she had not seen him moody before. She felt drops of rain on her face and hands, isolated drops like the beginning of a shower. She wanted it to rain. Then they would laugh and get wet and run in the rain. Or they might shelter under a tree. Let's go in here, she said, when they came to a little wood. There was a wood at the edge of the barley field, the sort of little wood he called a spinney. She was glad that she was wearing jeans for once because there were thick clumps of nettles they had to walk through at the edge of it, though under the trees the ground was clear. There was one great tree, an oak, with wide branches, and a dense canopy that would have held off the rain, if it had rained. They might have stood beneath that tree and stayed dry for quite a time, even if it rained hard. She said what a fine tree it was, and put out a hand to touch it. Do you see, Jonathan said, how old this tree must be? It must have grown big before the other trees grew around it, you can see that by the spread of its branches. When those branches formed it was growing out in the open, with light all around it.

He did not believe it was going to rain. He had not meant to go into the spinney but she ran ahead of him and he followed. He had not gone to the spinney since his father died. At first he had consciously avoided the spot, the scene of the first maumau, but so integral it was to the landscape, the little group of trees on a slight rise, visible from the house and from all across the farm, that in time it had become just a forbidden no-go place, as if it was an island of land that wasn't their land at all but someone else's, fenced off from him, and he would have been trespassing if he'd gone there. It must have changed, in all those years. It didn't feel changed. Except for the rooks. He did not think there had been rooks before, at least not in these numbers, loud overhead, their nests high in the ash trees – though of course the trees themselves must be higher or more broken than they had been then, some fallen and others grown. He didn't remember any rooks before. The trees were in leaf now in the summer, no sky to be seen above. Before, there would have been sky, or mist at least, not this close green light, this dappling over the ground, over the nettles, over her face. They came to the old oak. It was still a magnificent tree though it had recently lost a limb, a huge branch broken off on the ground and a tear still raw in the trunk above. She put her hands to the bark, tender as if she might heal it.

How many hundred years old do you think it is?

I don't know, he said, looking about him, looking at the ground where he had not looked for so long. He was here with Kumiko now. He wasn't that boy from before.

Could be three or four hundred years, he said. There used to be another big oak like this, he said, in the field, but it fell in a storm and when his father had it cut up they counted the rings in the stump and it was three hundred and fifty years old. So, it was all right to be here, with her. After so many years. Then, enough time had passed. He remembered how huge that other tree was on the ground, fallen in an autumn storm with still its weight of leaves on it that must have caught the wind; the excitement of climbing over and under and through a jungle of branches that had once stood high above them; the vastness of the exhumed roots and the fear of looking into the pit they had torn out of the ground; how deep it was, how it had already begun to fill with thick clayey water. The boys were told to stand back when their father went out with the men to clear the tree, cutting and pulling the branches that were heavy and green with leaf and like trees in themselves, trimming and stacking the big ones and piling the rest for burning, the trunk so wide that he had to bring other men with a saw powered by a tractor to slice it through. They found a fragment of lead wedged deep in the wood, he told her, so close to the heart of the tree that his father thought that it dated from the time of the Civil War. He had felt a kind of awe at that, as a seven-year-old, that there might have been a battle here. He tried to explain this, hearing himself as he spoke, speaking so calmly here in this place about these other things, at the same time hearing his father's voice in his mind, seeing his father's fingers, the roughened hand of a farmer, tracing the rings on the stump. There was fighting here, in the Civil War, his father had said, telling them about Roundheads and Cavaliers, he following Richard's lead and favouring the Cavaliers though he learnt when he was older that the Roundheads were meant to be better.

It didn't rain in the end. Or it hardly rained at all. Not so that they would have got wet. They might just have taken their walk, and not got wet, and got back home, and everything would have been fine. But she thought that it was going to rain and she made him come with her under the trees. The clouds grew dark, the spinney darker, and then there were big drops of rain falling on the leaves, and sometimes single drops that touched them, a sound like rain beginning, and just the beginning of that smell that the ground has when the rain touches it, but the shower stopped almost as soon as it began, and instead there was the smell of nettles crushed, a peppery salady smell, and she saw that he had picked up a stick and was thrashing at a clump of nettles, by where the branch had fallen, bashing them all down. Then he was kneeling in the nettles.

What's that?

It looks like a cross.

Why? Was someone buried here?

No. Not buried.

He saw just the tip of it at first. As if there was a grave there, two pieces of smooth wood neatly joined and set upright in the ground. So they had marked it, he thought. How strange, that someone had marked it.

If only it had rained, she would think, afterwards. If it had rained, they would have stood close, and sheltered.

And when enough rain had fallen they would have got wet even there beneath the tree, or running out from the trees, and noticed nothing but their wet selves with the rain falling about them.

This was where they had used to come. Where he had stood beside his father, with the dog. With Richard too, waiting for the birds to come in. Late on a winter's afternoon. His fingers chilling in woollen mittens. Getting cold, wanting to go in, but Richard was not going in, Richard was staying, and he had to do whatever Richard did, he would not have come out if Richard had not come out and now he had to stay and watch as Richard did, although he was so much younger and not ready to learn to shoot himself for some years yet; he stood still and chill beside his brother and his father and the dog, and felt the cold seep into him until it hurt and yet he didn't move an inch. And at last his father would raise the gun at the oncoming birds. Or on himself. Hard to believe, in this little wood, so very green and humming, with the rooks overhead, how bare it had been that day he saw him lying there. It was all covered over now, so many years' leaves fallen beneath the tree, layer upon layer, and grass, nettles impinging, spreading, tall, reaching for the light. There should have been no sign of what had occurred. No evidence. Any chance-scattered shot from that day also long covered over within the tree, so many rings deep.

That's not right, he said. It says 'Rosie'. That's not right.
   Who's Rosie?
   It's not right.
   What's not right?

Rosie was a dog, he said. Rosie was Billy's dog.

His hands and knees stung as he knelt to push aside the last of the nettles. Stung almost to numbness. He traced the letters that were amateurishly carved into the wood.

What could Billy have been thinking, to do that? Billy, the one who found him, that day. It was Billy who had brought the news home. Billy had come with the news, and their dog Jess, and Rosie too, he must have had Rosie with him, only Jess on the lead he had to put her on to bring her away. He had trusted Billy. Of all of them he had trusted Billy the most. So how could Billy have buried the dog here? And his mother, too? How could they do something so very – he looked for the word, holding himself back, holding emotion in check, choosing the plainest, the least expressive word that came to him – so puzzling, so very – inappropriate?

There had been no nettles then, in November. The nettles at that time of year had died back to ghostly stalks and the ground was brown with fallen leaves. Grey sky above the bare trees. Fog low across the fields.

This is where he was, you see. My father, I told you about my father. Well, this is where it happened.

They stood so still that sounds were loud, the birds, big black birds, cawing above them, then the sound of the Land Rover somewhere in the fields. Jonathan turned to find a way out of the trees. As if he had said nothing. As if nothing of importance had been said. And she had said nothing in response. And then when they came out into the sunshine, there was Richard driving along the track. He stopped and waved them over. Richard, looking so physical and sure, the sun on him, on his hair and his tanned arms with their rolled-up sleeves. He reached across to open the door. She got in while Jonathan let the spaniel jump up into the back. All so normal except she thought that they should have walked on, the two of them. It would have been better if they had walked.

He looked out of the open window as Richard drove, the track ahead, the spinney receding. The wide sky. Wide land. When he spoke his voice was flat, commonplace.

That old oak's still there.

It's lost a few branches these last years.

There's a grave underneath it.

Rosie's grave. Billy's dog, remember?

Yes, I remember Rosie.

Their words were hollow of meaning as if they needed translation.

I hadn't been there in years.

I go and shoot there sometimes. It's always been a good spot for pigeons. Dad used to go there, remember?

Yes I remember that too.

She sat in the centre seat of the Land Rover crushed between them, her knees to Jonathan's knees, Richard's hand against her knees as he reached to the gear stick.

There's a big rookery there now.

What was a rookery? She didn't know. They spoke across her as if she was not there.

It was so big, the sky. Empty. He felt the huge emptiness

weighing on them as if the longer they remained the less they would move, like Richard and his mother, held here on the flat. That was how it had always been. And now here was Kumiko beside him, and he could only make empty talk.

———

Later, when they were alone again, Jonathan said they had stayed at the farm long enough.

Let's go away somewhere, he said.

Where, she said, Paris?

He was thinking of the Lake District.

That's still England.

It's a different kind of England. And I always promised I'd take you there.

Because I read Wordsworth in my English lessons at school.

For other reasons too. Because it's wild and romantic. Because I don't have enough money for Paris until I'm paid for harvest. And when it rains in the Lakes it really rains.

Later, she would think that he was trying to save them. Whether from the past or the present she didn't know. She didn't think that he knew either. Only that they should go away from there for a time.

Out after dawn

Richard had noticed his wet boots. Probably there was wet on his face too, and in his hair. Richard was bigger than him, dark against the light, blocking his way to the light of the kitchen, or even upstairs, to safety, where he might have run into his room and held the door shut. The only place left for him to run to was his father's study, and that way he would not go.

Where were you?

When?

This morning, I looked in your room. Where were you?

Nowhere. I wasn't anywhere.

His brother had been still asleep when he went out. His mother must still have been asleep. He had heard his father go down the stairs to the kitchen, like on every morning, though this seemed earlier than every morning. Maybe that was only because there was so little light outside. It was November and the days were slow to start, and besides, there was fog. He had heard his father go out, the soft thud of the back door closing, seen through his bedroom window, which looked out at the back onto the yard, his father go out across the yard carrying his gun. The house was all asleep, though he had seen his father go out. He had taken off his pyjamas and thrown on yesterday's clothes which lay on the chair by his bed, thrown them on any-old-how, and his coat and his gumboots from the passage downstairs, and run out after him. No gloves. His fingers would be cold. No hat either. He had left behind the stillness of the house and run into the cold and stillness of the fields where his father had disappeared. The fog covered everything, caught and stilled it. Coated his skin and his hair with cold dew. He might have gone no further if he hadn't heard the shot.

You went out, Richard said. Where were you? He held his arm up tight behind his back until the pain stabbed through. Your boots are muddy. I've seen them, down there in the passage where you took them off. The mud's wet.

There was a time later when Richard would say, You saw. It was almost a statement by then and not a question, but even then Richard did not know what it was that he had seen. A year later, Richard was still asking him to tell, hating him for his secret, and he couldn't tell him because his secret didn't have any words to it, it was only the thing that he had seen. This time Richard didn't touch him. He looked. His look was so hard that it hurt. But he couldn't look away. He just stared back, and he didn't give in. He didn't speak a word, only let the tears make their way down to his clenched lips. He knew that it mattered. It mattered all the more because Richard thought their father was his, more his than Jonathan's, because everyone said that he looked like him, was the spitting image of him, because he was older and did everything first, was trusted with a gun and would be a farmer after him. Richard's father, not Jonathan's father. Yet Jonathan knew what he didn't.

Richard was right. He saw. What did he see? The fog, the plough, the spinney, the tree, his father's body. The leaves beneath him. The consequence of the shot. The dog. Then his mother's face as they sat on the sofa. Her lie. He tripped and fell, she said. He was climbing a fence in a field, and he must have tripped, and the gun went off. That made a different picture. He could see that picture, and he could see the other one, which was true, though nobody said it was true, he could only see it and not speak it. He had been seeing such things ever since: things that were and weren't true, the appearance of things and what was said to be the appearance of things and what was missing from the appearances. How the appearance could be empty. How what was present could show what was absent. That knowledge had become a part of him and all that he did. It went into his relationships with people and the world. It went into his photographs. Perhaps it was what made his photographs good, when they were good: not only what they call 'eye' or composition or technique, but his understanding of what was beneath, behind, not there. Where the shadows went and where shadows didn't fall.

———

There was this difference between himself and Capa. Capa had photographed the moment of death. The shot. A Republican soldier thrown back by the impact of the bullet, arms outstretched, rifle just let go. The most famous photo he ever took. (If the photograph was true, of course, if Capa, who somewhat invented himself anyway, who invented his name and the life that went with his name, if Capa had not somehow set up the shot which was so like a Goya, which might have been composed by Goya.) Jonathan saw the scene after the shot, but it was only the aftermath; the image imprinted on him but never exposed to the world.

Go-aan, you up there

Now Jonny was taking her off to the Lakes. He saw his mother drive them away then he walked across the yards to the barns; out of the back door, across the cobbles there and past the empty stables and the mounting block, past the old flint barn and through to the wide concrete yard and the new barns where the machinery was kept.

He had one of the lads working with him and they were servicing the combine. The combine came out once a year, and once it was out you didn't want to lose a minute of its working time. You wanted it to run without a fault twelve hours a day, if you could go that long, intensively over just a couple of weeks. You brought it out from the barn. You washed it down, vacuumed the drum, checked sieves, straw runners, knives, belts; tightened and oiled and replaced. You put your hand to a spanner, wrenched at a too-tight nut. Hammered out a bent piece of metal. The work was purposeful, physical, absorbing in its way. The sound of it clattered between all the hard surfaces of the yard. In an hour or so – longer depending on how much shopping she decided to do – she would be home from dropping them off.

When they came back from their holiday there would

be pictures. He could imagine how they would be. The girl on hilltops blown by the wind, her smile in the sunshine, her black hair across her face, her hand reaching to pull the hair back. Or perhaps there would be only rain. It was the Lakes they were going to, after all.

She was the only Japanese he had ever met. He had never known anything much about the Japanese apart from the war. Most of what he had come to know he had learnt from Jonny, from what he had said and from his photographs. When Jonny first came back from his travels there were so many photographs. It had been amazing to think that his brother had been making a living as a photographer. There were masses of prints, and then rolls and rolls of film that he had developed, and he had laid them out on the dining-room table. It was like the *National Geographic* spread there, so many places he'd been. All they'd seen at home till then were the war pictures that had made it to the papers; but Jonny had put those away somewhere, there weren't any of soldiers or fighting. There were others of Vietnam that made it look quite a nice place. Jonny said that Saigon was a much nicer place than you'd think. Old houses with balconies, wrinkled old ladies on the balconies smiling down, pretty girls – pretty as, prettier than, Kumiko. Of course there were the pictures of Kumiko. Jonny didn't say who she was at first. She was just this one Japanese girl smiling, in the city, on the beach, under the trees. He worked it out easily enough. Richard went in now and then when Jonny was sorting them. Jonny let him look at the prints and the contact prints and the slides, gave him a glass that he held unfamiliarly in his hand as he looked at the slides on the light box.

Who's the girl?

That's Kumiko.

She looks nice.

She is nice.

She had this big smile and she wore bright colours, appearing again and again here and there in the sunshine.

Maybe she'll come here in the summer. Then you and Mum can meet her.

He had envied his brother this girl, the apparent ease she felt with him in the pictures – or maybe that was what made him a good photographer, that he was a quiet sort of bloke who made people feel easy around him. Richard didn't know anything about photography but he thought that the pictures were good. Objectively, not just for himself. For himself, they were compelling. It meant something just knowing that they were there, present in the house, behind the dining-room door. All those places, the people, the girl; these pieces of his brother's life. When Jonny was gone to London for a few days, and his mother was in town shopping after taking him to the train, he went in and looked through the photos alone. Lucky little Jonny. There were other pictures he hadn't shown, pictures taken close, in black-and-white. Black-and-white showed contour and shadow, intimacy. He liked this girl in black-and-white. He looked for a long while. When he came out from the room his mother was home. He hadn't heard her coming in.

What were you doing? she said.

Just looking, he said, as if he had been caught doing something he shouldn't.

That wasn't the only time. He went in again after that. Early in the morning when no one else was up, he'd just walk into the room and see that the images were there. Jonny wasn't hiding them, after all. They were out there on the big mahogany table for anyone to see. Sometimes the door wasn't even closed.

What was the point of all these pictures? Was this work? This, Jonny's work? So many images, that was all they were; they had no purpose. There was the girl; she was nice. There were the war photos; he had seen the point of those, though Jonny said he wasn't going to take war photos any more. The rest of it didn't seem to be work but only life. The streets he passed through. The people who passed by. Tokyo. He didn't like the look of Tokyo. It was so crowded, so full of Japanese. Everyone said the Japs did terrible things in the war. They said his father had had a terrible time because of the Japs, though they never got round to explaining precisely what that meant. But the Japanese looked so neat in Jonny's pictures, in their business suits in front of shiny buildings, and the girl had this big smile.

So when the girl came he knew her already but he didn't know her at all.

She was small and poised and neat in her movements. A lightness to her that seemed very feminine. That made him feel heavy. Many of the pictures he had seen of her showed a house, a Japanese-style house, not one of those shiny modern ones. Was it her house, or Jonny's, or maybe some other place they went to, where Jonny took the pictures? It was a house made of wood with paper windows and sliding screens inside like paper walls. It was different from any house he knew. He felt that he would be clumsy in such a house. Must he bend his head to go through the doors? Would it shake to the tread of his feet or his touch?

Her voice was like that too. Soft, with a simplicity in it, but that might have been just the way she spoke English. When they went out in the Land Rover it had been difficult to hear what she said over the sound of the engine. He had to get her to repeat herself a couple of times. So he stopped, and shut off the engine, and then it was his voice that had seemed too loud, when they got out and he showed her everything. It had been nice to be showing her things. She asked if he had learnt his farming at college but he told her how he had just seemed to know some of it, from the beginning, how he must have learnt as a child when he used to go round the farm with his father, sitting where she did, sometimes getting out, sometimes just sitting and watching out of the passenger window, learning like that.

Oh that's nice, she said, I think that Jonathan doesn't remember his father very much.

Of course he remembered, he said.

He was bound to remember, wasn't he? Because he was older. That was what he said to her, taking the opportunity to set himself apart from his younger brother who had brought this girl here. But there was no more than a vague figure in his mind as he spoke, the memory of a man's big hands lifting from the steering wheel, pulling the handbrake, opening the door, of a tall man in a cap and a blue shirt or a worn tweed coat walking out away from him into the field. There would be a decision for a boy then, whether to watch or whether to run after, fitting his running steps to the man's slow strides. If you wanted to see how a crop was growing you didn't look only at the edge, on the headlands, but you walked in towards the centre of the field. You walked in and then about, this way and that, and stopped at different points. You looked where you knew the soil was light, and where it was heavier and where the water stayed. And the man did that, silent ahead of the boy – if the boy had followed and not only watched – always moving on ahead so that the boy would see his back and his hands more vividly than his face. Then he was back in the Land Rover, and if the boy had got out then the boy climbed in too while he waited, and there was that hand on the brake, on the gear, and the smell of the outside, and a little of the smell of the cigarettes that he smoked, which clung to his clothing, brought back into the cab. Of course, he told the girl. Yes, I remember him well. And so they got back in, where the doors on each side had been left open, and he put his own hand to the gear and the brake, and they drove on.

People said he was like him. He didn't know about that. Physically he was like him; anyone could see that from family photos. Jonny didn't resemble him at all. But Jonny was the one who had gone looking while he kept to the farm. Jonny had gone to Asia and to war, like their father. He had stayed at home and worked the farm like their father. There was no telling which one of them had come closest.

His mother was home. They had an everyday lunch like they usually did when it was only themselves at home. Bread and cheese. Not much to say. The radio, the news, the weather forecast. Dry in Norfolk; rain in the north-east. It didn't sound good for the Lakes.

Did they say when they'd be back?

They weren't sure.

Better that they didn't come back, not for some time at least. Perhaps the weather would clear, in a day or two. When there was rain in the Lakes the cloud came down and there was nothing to see. He imagined them walking in cloud across the Lakeland hills, seeing nothing, the girl's red coat showing at a distance, Jonny opaque beside her, the path fading into the mist before them. After lunch, he would go out where it was flat and bright. His mother would take her gloves, her secateurs and her trug, and go to the garden. Everything would be normal, as it had always been, or as it had been these last few years, since he had been working the farm and since Jonny went away. It was the start of July. It was a day like the days when they first came home from school for the summer holiday. When he went away to school he had wanted to come home to a place where nothing changed. That was how he had liked it. That was still how he liked it. Fixed. He remembered how it was when he came home from school. The place had to be the same place that he had remembered each day when he was away. He would come back from school and look at the room where he and his brother slept, or, later when they slept in separate rooms, his room alone, and then go downstairs and outside, walk the bounds of the place and check that everything was still there and nothing had been moved, and no one had come and meddled in it. He would go to the garden where his mother came out with her trug and her secateurs, or where she knelt weeding, and climb the walnut tree from which he and his brother could see everything at once, all around: their mother, the garden, the hedge around the garden, the house, the drive, the fields, the church, the village, other fields and woods, and the sky over it all.

Those first holidays when they came home from school the two brothers were close, though at school they had been apart, divided by age and dormitories and forms. They came home a pair and changed out of their uniforms and left them on the floor for their mother to pick up, and wore their home clothes, and often Jonny's clothes were clothes that used to be his but that didn't matter because they were anybody's clothes, the clothes of a boy at home. Jonny walked behind him as he made his tour of the place. Jonny climbed the tree with him. A rope hung from the lowest branch of the tree so that they could climb. It had hung there all through the term untouched, and now they climbed it. Their father had put the rope there, and tied knots in it, one big one at the base and two others on the way up to make the climb easy. Jonny could climb the rope as easily as Richard could. They climbed onto the branch and along to where it joined the trunk and sometimes up onto one of the adjoining branches and watched. They spent hours in those first few days that they were home in the tree watching their world, astride the branch or with their backs to the trunk, watching their mother gardening, watching who came and went. They were home, but the walnut was home within the home. Like the place you called home when you played It. Where you could be seen but not be caught. Where all three of them could be seen. Because they each of them knew that any day any one of them might walk out of the house and disappear.

The leaves of the walnut were long and oval and green. They had a strong dark smell. The smell was there in the tree even when the leaves were green. It would be stronger when they fell and blackened and grew greasy in the autumn and Billy swept them up. In the tree it was as if you could smell that blackening already though it was summer. Perhaps it was the sun shining through the leaves that made the smell come out. It you looked up through the tree the leaves were a bright apple-like green despite their odour, and the branches between them were elephant grey but smooth, smoother than elephant skin would be, if you were to touch and climb an elephant. If he stood on one of the lower branches he could put two hands to the one above and pull himself up, rest his tummy on the branch, lift a leg astride it while Jonny stayed below as he wasn't tall enough to reach. From that point the branches were more closely spaced so he could go higher. Don't go any higher, Jonny said, from his safe branch below. It makes the tree move when you go higher, I can see the top of the tree moving, it's scary, you'll fall. It's fine, he said, finding a place to put his foot, lifting himself up one last branch.

I can see everything from here.

The top of the tree swayed just so little beneath his weight. He could see clear in every direction. He was like a hawk on a telegraph pole, looking down. Sharp as a hawk, watching for movement below. There was his mother talking to Billy who was getting the lawn-mower out. There was Mrs T coming on her bicycle up the drive. There was Jackson's little grey tractor out in their fields where he was topping the field edges before harvest. The fields were still their fields though Jackson worked them. Now Billy was pulling at the cord of the mower. The mower was starting with a puff of blue smoke. His mother was walking towards the tree across the lawn. Mum. Look, Mum. See where I am. She didn't hear him over the sound of the mower.

Later he took his father's old binoculars and put a string on them and climbed up there again, on his own this time, and tied the binoculars to a small branch so that they would be there whenever he went to his perch.

I'm like a hawk, he said to his mother. I climb high up the tree.

She didn't know how high he meant.

I see everything. I watch you from high up. I see Billy. I see Jackson. I see Jackson's men. I see the people who come to visit. I see you talking to them, wherever you are.

He thought a lot about hawks. There were sparrow-hawks along the roads and kestrels, and sometimes bigger birds, buzzards, and once he saw what he thought was a harrier off the marshes, identifying it later from a book. He watched them through the binoculars. He saw how still they could be, holding as still sometimes in the sky as on a pole. How quickly they swooped when they saw whatever it was they saw moving on the ground. How ruthless they were.

When Jackson's men brought the combine out, he swooped down.

Mum, can we go and see?

Yes, if the men'll have you.

But sometimes still he did not like to see Jackson on the fields. And nothing that Jackson did went on without his seeing, at least when he was home. Once he came home and saw that Jackson had changed the fields. He did not like it when Jackson did such things.

It was in the autumn and the winter that that sort of thing happened, when the fields were bare. It must have been when they came home for one autumn half-term or the Christmas holiday. The first thing that went wrong was that Billy had removed the rope. He found Billy working in the shed. He shouted at Billy. Billy, you shouldn't have done that. An eleven- or maybe twelve-year-old scolding a man in his sixties; he would be in trouble for that later. Billy said that the rope was rotten, he took it away because it was dangerous. But you can't do that, Billy. Daddy put it there.

He could climb the tree now anyway because he had grown tall and strong enough to jump up and grab the first branch and swing himself up. And he could get Jonny up first by letting him stand on his shoulders. They could get up without any rope. Jonny had got bigger too, and bolder, so they both climbed up high to where the tree swayed. There was the garden below, empty since Billy was in the shed and his mother was indoors, no one about to see them, though they were so high and though most of the leaves had gone from the tree. The only people to be seen were Jackson's men, and the fields looked different. Crikey, no, they can't do that! He held the binoculars to his eyes. What is it? Jonny said. Let me see. But already he had let the binoculars drop on their string and was heading down, swooping, branch to branch, even as Jonny took them up to see for himself.

Wait for me.

Jonny was behind, and slow. He was already down on the ground.

Wait. It's too high. I can't get down.

Jonny was scared. He had not climbed so high in the tree before.

Yes you can.

He was running, out from the gate and into the fields, across the stubble. Jackson's men had a digger there to dig up the hedges, a huge digger of a kind he had never seen before, with caterpillar tracks. The digger was so big and noisy that they didn't hear him shouting. They didn't even see him until he picked up a stone and threw it. It was a sharp broken flint and he threw it hard. He was aiming at the machine not at the men but one of the men was hit. The man put up his hand to his head and there was blood. He turned and ran for home.

How could you let him do it? he shouted at his mother. She was in the kitchen as usual, and Jonny was in there, sitting at the table with a glass of milk. Jonny had got down almost OK, only when he got to the bottom branch he jumped wrong and landed badly, twisting his ankle. He was probably going too fast, panicking, that was like Jonny. Maybe it hurt a lot. Maybe it wasn't really so bad. Maybe he would have pulled himself together and come after, if there had been any hope of catching up. Or maybe he didn't want to be implicated. He could see Jonny had been crying. He didn't cry. He was only angry. Angry and hard and sharp and dry-eyed like a hawk. Angry at Jackson and angry at his mother for letting Jackson do what he had done to their land, his father's land. How could you let that happen?

It's how things are, his mother said. He's just a farmer doing his job. That's what farmers do nowadays. Later she drove him over to Jackson's to apologise. He did what she said. He got out of the car and stood at Jackson's front door and said the words but he kept his fists clenched and his eyes dry.

After that Jackson wouldn't have him out on the farm, or not for a year or two, until he was old enough to show that he was sensible and could do a job of work as a barn boy. Billy got a new rope and put it up on the tree, and he got some planks and made a lookout platform, but Richard hardly ever used it. Jonny took to going there with a book to read. It was his place after that, a place for little boys and not for hawks.

———

Of course, his mother was correct. Jackson was only doing what everyone was doing then. A farmer could not afford to be sentimental about land. He learnt that as he learnt to farm. Eventually he would come to grub out more hedges, cut down more trees and fill more ponds than Jackson had, to work every fertile square yard of his soil. It was like she said, it was what a farmer did. He'd been to college and it was what they taught, and it was what you learnt when you bought the machinery that was bigger than the machinery had been before, so that you could work with fewer men and bigger fields. And if you didn't, well, you couldn't be competitive, could you? You wouldn't survive.

Only by that time she had changed her mind. Perhaps he would never do quite right before her. She was watching as he took the farm back, and he was failing her, as if he was doomed to fail before her eyes. Perhaps it would have been better if she had not kept it for him so that he had to follow, looking like his father, in his father's footsteps, resented by her for being what he was being which was only after all what he was and what his father had been before. Bit by bit, he took the farm back, and though it was what she had been waiting for all these years he had the feeling that she didn't want it to happen any more. He had begun with the barn, which he needed to put his machinery in. He emptied it of its junk. He rid it of the fantail pigeons that nested in the rafters, put it back how his father would have had it. She had loved the fantails, which had come as a pair and had bred into a flock over the years, ornamental white birds, not wood pigeons, that used to perch exquisitely in the sunlight on the crest of the roof, or coo and strut and display on the ground of the yard. She asked if they couldn't have stayed. They're the sort of birds that live in dovecotes, not barns, he said. Look at the shit on the floor. If his father had been around, there wouldn't have been a single pair of fantails nesting in the barn. But his father hadn't been around. It was she who had let them colonise the place. We're a farm, Mum. We're growing food for people to eat. In this context they're just a kind of vermin. It hadn't been his choice to have the farm; it was she who had hung on to it. How could she then not let him farm it as he saw fit?

So one evening he closed the big barn doors when the birds were roosting, and the next morning he went out with his gun.

Don't come, Mum. Don't look. Don't see this.

And he went in and closed the door behind him and shot a dozen birds in the fluttering space, and only then let the rest of the flock escape. The door thrown open, light flooding in, a rush of wings overhead. The dead birds heaped in a barrow, to be taken and buried or burned on the fire. Blood red on white feathers. His look hard on them, the hope in it that he had killed enough so that the others wouldn't come back. If his mother had had her way, she would have given the whole farm over to her fancy birds, let the hedges grow and fall across the ditches, the bramble and blackthorn spread and tangle into thickets, those roses with the French names ramble out from the garden over everything.

One day in the winter that followed, he started on the cowshed. Only himself and his mother at home now since Jonny was away, and he found it hard, in the quiet of the house, to be idle. When there was no activity Jonny's absence became all the more noticeable, and with it the implication of his own continued presence, his permanence in the place. This particular day it was raining heavily. The ground outside was too sodden to work and would likely be so for some days to come. Clearing the cowshed was something to do. No urgency to the job, only that the building was derelict. The cowshed like the old barn had stood empty for fifteen years, but there was nothing he needed it for. It was obsolete as well as derelict, though it had only been put up in the 1930s, the modern building seeming emptier than the old one could ever have been.

The metal door rattled open onto a clanging void, concrete floor, tin roof, railed pens, feeding troughs, lengths of pipe that once held rat poison. There was no other debris there save what had been used for the cows. Even the murky air had a different quality from the air of the barn, a stale but still acrid odour come of the long disintegration of shit and straw, which had seemed to impregnate even the metal. He put on overalls and gloves and tied a handkerchief across his face, and spent a day clearing, putting what might be sold at auction or for scrap out into the yard where the rain washed it down. His mother saw it there and came out to see what he was doing, wearing a big black oilskin because the rain was hard, came into the shed and pushed back the dripping hood to look about her. How long since she had last been in there? Not since the cows left, perhaps, when it was a bright space soft with straw and warmed by the beasts. But the electricity had been cut off long ago, wires hanging loose, overhead sockets dangling smashed bulbs. She went to push the door fully back and let in more light, of whatever light there was outside on a day like that, but the door was stuck in its runners, it wouldn't go any further. She was coughing in the churned-up, sour-smelling dust, holding her hand to her mouth.

What are you doing?

Clearing.

Why?

To take it down. We don't need it any more. We can put up a modern grain store instead.

And he said he would take down the cart barn too.

But it's a lovely old cart barn.

But that's what it is. It was built for carts.

Didn't she see, the point wasn't the past but the present?

You and your bright new toys, she said, turning away and back out into the rain.

As if a man was still only a boy.

It slowly came to him, how they had changed. She might have been thinking these thoughts for a while, but he hadn't noticed. He didn't much notice that sort of thing – but maybe other people didn't either, not when it was a question of the people they lived with. The people you lived with you took for granted, you didn't expect them to change or even to get any older, not visibly, only infinitesimally and unseen from day to day and yet each morning looking the same. She had once read a book about a silent spring. There had been a time when everyone had seemed to be reading that book but that time was passed. It said how chemicals were destroying nature. He thought, they would have got over it by now, and besides, things like DDT had been banned; modern science had come a long way since then. But the idea was still alive in her, making her afraid of what he did. She would say, I worry, you know, about the future. She would come downstairs in the mornings. The birds, she would say, did you hear the birds this morning? That lurking possibility in her, each morning, that this day of all days the birds might not have sung. Or if they sang today, that their numbers were reducing, numbers of buzzards or sparrows, or of returning swallows, the house martins' nests in the eaves not filled this year, not replaced, the lapwings not come to the fields. She spoke as if his work was a threat to them all, the everyday work of the farm some kind of violence. These sprays you use, I can't stand the smell of them. She took up his overalls in her yellow rubber gloves and put them into the washing machine. The smell clings, she said, even when they're washed.

Only it didn't. His overalls when they came out of the machine were clean. If anything, they smelled of detergent, since she put in so much. He thought that she must have imagined the smell, on them and possibly sometimes even on himself.

He saw grey in her hair, lines on her face, a particular fine vertical pair of lines on her brow, above her nose. They must have been there for a while. Criticism in them. Some hardening where he used to think that she was soft.

Why don't we have cows again, like we used to? We could use the shed. You haven't torn it down yet.

He had the shed pulled down.

It was she who had sold the cows. The hurt was still there in him. The boy's white knuckles in the grown man.

The herd

He had understood what was happening the moment he saw the cattle truck. He saw from the landing window as he was coming down the stairs. Ran then, down and along the passage and out the back door. There was his mother standing with some papers in her hands. The driver of the truck had opened the doors, set out a ramp.

No. You can't do that. He ran and tore the papers from her hands and threw them down in the mud of the yard. The driver turned and looked at him, and he saw through into the interior of the truck, the empty space striped with light waiting for the cattle to fill it. Hands grabbed him and held him tight, his mother's hands holding him back with more force than she had ever held him. She pulled him back tight against her. Her arms folded about him like iron. No. He twisted about and screamed and kicked at her legs. Then after a while he stilled.

Jonny was standing beside them now. Quiet, only watching. He felt Jonny's quiet. It made him quiet. He wasn't going to be babyish beside his little brother. His mother's arms softened about him but didn't remove themselves. When he gave a shiver that might have been the beginning of an escape, they tightened again.

A boy should not run mad into a herd of cattle, even when they seemed at their most docile, driven out from the shed towards the ramp. He knew that. He should not scatter them or panic them into the unpredictable. He knew these things. His father had told him such things. When his father had told him things like that, the knowledge had seemed special, intended for him man to man, making him a man even when he was a boy. Whoa, go-aan then. Matthew the cowman was herding the animals as if there had been no commotion, as if he wasn't there and had never screamed, so calm that it was as if the animals had not seen him either. Matthew walked forward slowly behind the herd with his arms outstretched, speaking long low vowels. On the other side Billy and the driver did the same. The rusty-coloured cattle moved with slow inevitability towards the ramp. Go-aan, you, up there. The first one or two hesitated, looked about them. That's right. Go-aan. As they reached the ramp the animals behind them seemed to flow together, becoming one softly heaving mass within the prison space of the truck.

The arms were still there, tight about him.

They're Daddy's cows. His voice was thin, high-pitched, strange even to himself.

Not really, they weren't ever really Daddy's cows, you know that. They were Great-Uncle Ralph's, Ralph's herd. Daddy only kept them on for Matthew's sake.

Again her arms tightened as he struggled against her. So? We can keep them too.

She bent down in front of him where she could look into his eyes, but not letting go, her two hands to his upper arms. She spoke gently, reasonably. But, darling, we can't. You know Jackson's running the farm now, not us, and Matthew's getting too old to deal with them anyway.

Fuck, he said. Fuck. To her face.

The men were putting a chain across the back of the truck. They were closing the doors, folding up the ramp. Through the openings between the slats of the truck he could see the cattle, their reddish haunches and sides; their faces turned, rubbed against, looking out. The noise they made seemed not to be the noise of individual animals but the prolonged moan of one single sad trapped beast. He cried for the great beast. He cried more than he had ever cried at any other time. He wrenched himself away now as the arms had gone limp, and ran behind the truck as it started up. He went on running as it bumped away along the drive. He ran with flailing arms, fell, picked himself up and ran again, the tears streaming, a cut on his knee running with blood.

His mother ran after him but he was too fast for her. Maybe she was letting him run, letting him run it out of him. He could come to no real harm on this track. But when she finally reached him, at the gate by the road, he did not so much as let her look at his bleeding knee. Even as she crouched before him he turned away. Tight, shaking, tear-drenched face averted, fists clenched white, he brushed past her soft hand and her skirt and walked back towards the yard.

There, boy, there. There it is. There you go. Old Matthew put two hands to his shoulders and spoke in the same tone that he used for the cattle. Matthew too had tears in his eyes.

The smell of them lasted in the fields for months. In the empty shed it remained for days and weeks and years, even in the cold when other smells faded, the smell or the memory of the smell, in dung drying to pale flaking crusts on the concrete floor. He used to go every now and then into the old cowshed, where no one else ever went, not pushing back the big door, he wasn't strong enough to do that – and besides, it made such a noise rolling back on its runners that people would know he was there – but softly in by the small door at the side of it where the catch was broken. Once he was inside he had left the people and the world outside. He closed his eyes and knew again the warmth of the cows in their wire and concrete stalls, their lowing and shuffling, the green splatter of their shit. He was crouching safe between their red-brown flanks.

———

No one would find him. Not even Jonny, though he heard him calling in the yard.

Where are you? That one of the calls of the younger brother: Where are you, Wait for me, Let me come, Can I play too … There was always a choice to be made for him in those calls: would he answer, would he let him in or not? No. He would not let him in here. This must be his place alone.

Where are you? I know you're somewhere around here. Then the creak of the metal door pushed open. Jonny was cleverer than he thought. Or it was his own fault, he must have not quite closed the door, Jonny must have seen it just so slightly open. A bar of cold light entered the grey of the shed. There was no time to move, only the cows to hide him.

What are you doing? Jonny stood before him at the opening to his stall.

None of your business. Go away.

The cows were quite gone. Only their dried-up smell remained. Jonny stood where they had been.

But there's nothing here.

Go away.

He went on standing there looking puzzled. He didn't even start to move.

See this, Richard said, and pointed at a little pile of blue-dyed grain.

What's that?

That's poison, he said. It's called Warfarin. Matthew put it out for the rats. It doesn't matter about the rats now so I've been collecting it up. If you come in here again I'll poison you.

Still Jonny stood there, wide-eyed now. But it looks like grain, he said.

It is grain, but it's been soaked in poison. That's why they make it blue, so you can tell the poisoned grain from the good stuff. The rats can't tell because Matthew puts it out in pipes on their runs, and they run through in the dark and eat it because it smells like any other grain, and maybe it tastes like any other grain because they come back for more, and because sometimes Matthew puts sugar with it to make it sweet. And when they've eaten enough they go and die in their holes. They die, and dry out, from the inside out, like mummies, I've seen.

Jonny had taken a step closer.

Didn't you hear what I said? If I put it in your food you won't smell it or taste it, any more than a rat does.

It's blue. I'll see it, won't I? I don't eat in the dark.

How long?
As long as it takes

It rained in the Lakes, and the hills were grey. When the rain stopped and the sun came out the hills were purple and the sky was blue. Jonathan took pictures in black-and-white. Why do that, she wanted to say, when there are these colours? It's the colours that make the place so beautiful. But he was seeing the curves of the hills and the sheen of the lakes, and the way the light came between the clouds and fell across them. It made her aware of things like that, travelling with Jonathan. She started to see what he saw, what she might not have seen for herself. She began to see where he would take his pictures – or if not where, then when. What concerned him might be the light or the shadows, not the colours or even the forms. The moving things, the moment, the places between, and how he might catch them.

One day they climbed a mountain into a big wind. She stood at the top with her arms out like an aeroplane falling forward into the wind but the wind kept her upright. She could see the horizon where the wind came from, and a lake dark in the valley deep below, and cloud moving through the valley. She called to Jonathan, her words carried back on the wind, and he came and stood there too and put out his arms. Then the wind blew the cloud up from the valley. They could feel the cold and the moistness of it before it reached them, swirling up and hiding the lake and then all the land below until there was no view any more but only cloud, and he pulled her close and put his arms around her.

Do you still love me? she said. She said it again, loud. She had to speak loudly as the wind took her words away.

Of course I love you.

Do you love me as much as you did in Japan?

Of course.

Sometimes I think it's different, now you're in England.

Why should it be different?

His face was cool, damp with the mist.

Just that things are different here.

Maybe it's you that's different.

Wind. Cloud. Words blown about in the cloud. He. She. One of them. Different.

Maybe he was no different, she thought in that moment. Only the place. That was what was wrong. What seemed free in Japan was no longer freedom once he was home.

She remembered why he had left Japan, or why he said he was leaving. I'm not Japanese, am I? I'm outside of it all. I can only watch and not touch.

But that's your job, she said, that's being a photographer. That's who you are. You watch. You look. You see, and you show us things about the world we live in that we don't know we've seen.

It seemed OK there, in Tokyo, that he was doing that.

And besides, you touch me, she said. You touch me lots.

He laughed then, as if she was right and he was silly to have had that idea.

OK, he said, maybe you're right, but I still have to go home, for a while at least, and you can come too, and then we'll go from there.

The walk took them on along a ridge and through bare stretches of land. They had to watch the ground carefully for the path. It was only a thin beaten track that had been made by the people who had walked it before. No one but the two of them up there that day but she was aware of all the others, walking that path looking for the cairns, or some of them building the cairns, picking up stones to mark where they had been so that other people could see and follow. If it hadn't been for the cairns they might have got lost, up there on the top of the mountain. She went behind him in the mist, his dull green coat that blended with the rocks. She had come all that way to be with him but he receded before her, camouflaged in his green coat, closed into his thoughts. She ran to catch up with him.

Wait for me, she said. I don't want to lose you up here.

———

There was a time in Tokyo when he showed her his photos from the war. They were horrible pictures that she didn't like to see and liked less to remember, but all the same she could not pull herself away from them. He gave her a magnifying glass and let her see all of them, the contact prints, the pictures that were not published as well as the ones that were, standing behind her, watching her look, as if each of the pictures was a confession that he had to have her see, showing her things that she did not want to see, that he did not want ever to have seen himself, as if he thought that she would not want to see him if he had seen those things. That's who I am, he said. A spectator. A taker of pictures. He said that he had felt cold, taking those photos, even when he had been sweating with fear. And it was cold of him, to show them to her. I did not mean to be cold, he said. It's something in me.

No, she said. It's only the camera. You put the camera in front of your eyes.

It was raining in the south also when they went back to the farm. In the south rain was different, Kumiko saw, not a force any more, only rain. Claire said that it had been fine most of the time they had been gone. It had started to rain just a day or two before. Grey rain. The fields a dull matt gold because of the wet. More rain waiting in the sky in darker bands of cloud. Colour flat, shapes flat, lines horizontal. Like somebody's painting she had seen once, only she couldn't think whose.

So good to have you back, Claire was saying. Was it lovely there? Did you have good weather? She had picked them up at the station. She had not known until she saw them how happy she would be to have them back. They were driving home through the lanes. She drove a little carelessly, looking across to Kumiko sitting in the front, glancing back to Jonny behind, chattering because they were quiet, hoping to see from their faces that they had had a happy time together. Like when Jonny was a boy and she used to pick him up from somewhere, hoping things had gone well.

It's been beautiful here till now, she said. Just till this

last couple of days. Richard's fretting of course. This weather's not good for him. He was all ready to get the combine out before this rain.

There were puddles along the road, the hedges sagging, the nettles on the verges limp with the moisture. She had to brake suddenly at a bend when they met a car coming too fast from the other direction, stop and reverse to where there was width in the road to let the other car pass. Yet she went on talking, feeling the need to talk.

Do you know, we came off the road just there once, Charlie and I?

She remembered how happy two people could be, but how unhappy also.

Just here, into a snowdrift. That was in the dreadful winter of 1947. You can't imagine how high the drifts were, looking at it all now. We had to leave the car and walk home.

You never told us that before, Mum.

Didn't I?

He was looking out at the rain. All day on the train they had been looking out at rain. There had been so many homecomings, so many times that they had been this way. His parents before he was born, walking in the snow. Or a boy riding in the grain cart, on that same sharp bend. Two boys, one bigger than the other, laughing. The cart swinging round the bend and the surface of the heap shifting, the smaller boy sinking down open-mouthed into a golden quicksand of wheat, feet, legs, body, fear of drowning, grain in his mouth, gripping hard to the hard sides of the cart, coming home with his eyes red and running. Hay fever, his mother would say. From all the dust.

All the times we've driven this road, you never told us.

I'm sure I must have. You've just forgotten.

Perhaps she had told him, he couldn't be sure.

This year he had offered to drive for Richard. He didn't think they would let a boy ride in the cart nowadays. He would have to take care on the bend all the same, take it slowly so that the grain didn't spill.

Well, it was a long time ago, she was saying. They were close to the house. Through breaks in the hedge on each side of the road came glimpses of Richard's sodden wheat.

The accident had been her fault, even if Charlie was driving. They had walked home cold in the snow and the dark, huddled by the Aga when they got in, not speaking, each of them separate and alone. They had had a row. It was because of something she had said that Charlie had put his foot down too hard and come off the road. Always it seemed to have been a question of what she was saying and what Charlie was not saying, though it was what Charlie did not say that mattered more than anything she could put into words. She had said what she had said because of Charlie, because of whatever it was in him which was constantly with them and made her afraid. That was before family. Family had been meant to warm them. To fill the silences. Children to bring happiness, to make a way to the future. She was glad that there would be family now, this summer at least, her boys together, this nice girl here, Jonny helping out for these few weeks.

She recognised the trees that marked the site of the farm

from a distance. Then the house came into view, with the barns around it, looking square in the centre of its land. She remembered which painter it was. It was Mondrian, when he painted landscapes before he painted abstracts. She and Jonathan had seen an exhibition of his paintings in Tokyo. It seemed an age ago that they did that. It made her sad, that it seemed so long ago. She thought, Mondrian was from Holland and Holland was flat; maybe you felt like painting abstracts if you lived in flat landscape like this.

She had thought the paintings were cold. Jonathan had liked them for their form and restraint. She closed her eyes. It had been a long journey. She sat beside Claire in the front, Jonathan in the seat behind her where she could not see him. Wait for me, she might have said, running after him up there on the mountain. Wait, I don't want to lose you here. Now let me have a turn, she would say. Let me take a picture now. And he takes the camera from about his neck. And she takes it, hard and black and smooth in her cold wet hands. She holds it by the strap. She does not put the strap safe over her head, but only holds it, holds and swings it, and hurls the camera out into the mist. A black box turning, falling unseen to the lake below.

Here we are, home, Claire was saying.

They turned off the lane into the drive. There was the old iron gate wedged open. Probably the gate didn't move. She never saw anyone try to move it. There was grass tangled about the base of it that must have grown there for years. Then they were past the gate and driving up to the house. There were the tall straight hedges like walls, and beyond them the garden itself. The garden didn't look so beautiful as it had when she had left only two weeks before. Because of the rain, of course, but also because the roses, which she thought of as Joséphine's roses but which were not Joséphine's roses at all, had finished flowering.

I've put you both in the spare room this time. Take your things up and then come down and I'll make you some tea.

She had gone to the fishmonger's before she went to the railway station. They ate fish only when she had been into town, which she didn't do often when there was just herself and Richard in the house; when it was just the two of them she tended to make do with what she could get in the village. Now that she had everyone home, she cooked with care. Fish pie. Family supper. Once the work started meals would be functional and hurried, left a long time keeping warm in the bottom of the oven or even taken out to the field. You used to make this, Mum, when we came home from school. Did I? Yes, I suppose I did. I'd make it beforehand, so I could just heat it up when we'd driven home. She had forgotten. It was one of those rituals, of coming home from school, when the things that were done filled in for all that had not been said, the missing and the separation. This was like the days when they came home from school for the summer. July weather, two boys home, the summer holidays stretching ahead. Raspberries from the garden, only now they would have lost their flavour a bit after the rain. Meringues and cream. They had always liked her meringues, and they were so easy to make, overnight in the Aga, these too ready before the holidays began. When the meal was over and they were watching television she took the dog out. The dog snuffled off into the dark and she followed. There was no moon. The night was dank, still. This stillness was no good for Richard. It was warmth and wind, drying air, that Richard needed. She walked to the border before the hedge, where there was only a thin scent from the tobacco plants. They needed warmth to bring out the scent. She had planted them for warm nights, aromatic flowers to draw moths in the dusk. She looked back on the façade, so formal and regular with the wisteria trained across it. There were lights in the sash windows all along, in the hall and in the sitting room downstairs, and on the landing above and in the bedrooms to each side.

Such a pretty façade. The setting for the illusion that was to have been her work. Here, Charlie, here we are, a happy family, two sons, my darling, one dark, one fair, like ourselves, and our fields stretching about us. Not quite all the land you can see from here, because the skies and the horizons are big. But enough. And we shall have a beautiful garden with hedges tall about it. And how they will love this place. They will be rooted here, in this piece of land which has been in the family for so long, in this place and in the past.

Jonny had not said how long his girl would stay. She had been careful not to ask. He had committed himself to working on the farm through the harvest. She supposed that Kumiko would be with them that long at least. Then they were to go away, travelling in Europe, until when she did not know. She hoped that he would bring her back after.

It was surprising, how things turned out. It occurred to her how many plants she had in the garden that came from Japan, which had crept in without her thinking where they were from. She had been coming to love things Japanese even when she had thought she disliked them. She had come to realise it only by their names: her tree peonies and cherry trees, the *autumnalis* that flowered so kindly through the winter; *Skimmia, Pieris, Chaenomeles*, evergreen shrubs that flowered in the early spring. Others, probably, that she hadn't thought of. The wisteria itself, though she regretted sometimes that she had not put in the Chinese variety, which she now thought more elegant. A deep pink camellia. Joséphine had a *Camellia japonica*. There was a painting of one by Redouté in the Fitzwilliam in Cambridge, Redouté who had painted the plants in Joséphine's collections, whose paintings were almost more famous than the flowers.

He's there in the field again.

Who?

Richard, of course.

This morning they woke in the same room, Jonathan in the spare bed beside her.

He's always there, in the mornings, when I look out.

The talk the night before had been all about where they had been in the Lakes and what they had done, what hills they had climbed, the boat they took out on Windermere. And you, she had asked Richard, what have you been doing? Waiting, he said. Watching the weather. Watching the crop. (And now in the evening, she had thought, watching the rest of us talk.)

So there he was again in the early morning, out in the field beyond the hedge. Watching.

In Tokyo Jonathan was the Englishman. She thought at first that there was Englishness in everything that he did. But Richard was more English than he was. Or maybe it was only the surface that made a man English or not English. Once you knew him well you didn't see that any more.

Claire said that Richard looked like his father. Handsome and fair-haired and blue-eyed. English.

All she knew about Jonathan and Richard's father was how he died. That was all he had become. Whoever he was, was hidden behind it. So much of him hidden, even here in this house and in his family. Maybe his death had been in him years before, when he was alive as well. Maybe Claire knew that all the time. That was why she was so careful of Richard.

How long shall we stay now? she asked Jonathan.

I don't know, he said. As long as it takes. It depends on the weather.

And when the weather's good, how long then?

A week or two. You don't mind that, do you, being stuck here? You could go somewhere if you like, go up to London on your own?

No, she said. That's fine. I like it here.

It used to be his time alone, this time of day. His mother was never an early riser. When they were boys Jonny went out before him one day and never told where he went. Now he was the one who always woke first. But the girl was awake. The days began very early now in midsummer. She woke as early as he did, and she came to the window to draw back the curtain and look out. When he saw her there the first time he had thought that it must be the jet lag, that she was on Japanese time and that was why she was up. Not any more. And she was not alone in her room any more, Jonny was with her, and still she woke early and went to the window. She must just be a morning person. He liked that thought. He was aware of her waking presence within the house as before he had been aware of her pictures on the table.

On the headland where he had walked into the field the crop was thin and still a little green but here at the heart of the field it was ripe and dense. The wheat looked good this year, this his fourth harvest and the yield would be the best, if only this rain would stop and he could get it in. The stalks were strong and the leaf blades showed no sign of discolouration. The heads were thick. He broke one off, separated the sheath to look at the grain in it, rolled the kernel out from the husk, put it to his teeth. Ready to go. Only the ground was wet, slippery underfoot. There was water lying on the tracks and on the tramlines through the crop. He did not like to see water lying this time of year.

He had checked the barometer before he went out. He did that every morning, and again at night when he came in and sometimes again when he went to bed. A habit of the house. The barometer hung in the hall where you passed it whenever you went in or out, or just when you went upstairs or into the office or the sitting room. It had hung there so long that it did not look as if it would bear to be moved. It was an antique barometer, early nineteenth century or something, the kind that was made to look like a miniature piece of furniture, of polished walnut, but pieces of veneer flaked off in places, its face stained, the tiny glass flask that held the mercury slightly askew in its metal clamps. He didn't know why they had bothered to make it decorative when it was a functional thing, but he liked its being like that. He liked its being there. It must have been there long before his father. It would have been there for his father's uncle Ralph. It might have been there before Ralph too, already there when Ralph came to the house, for all the farmers before him, so many men checking it before they went out, walking across the hall, tapping the barometer, turning then away from the front door to go down the passage to the kitchen, take a cap from a hook and go out at the back into the yard. So many of them, over the years, repeating the same damn pattern. Pressure low. No change from the day before. The radio forecast had said the same. Risk of showers in late morning, sometimes heavy. The sky was a uniform grey. When he first looked out its colour hadn't told him anything. It looked the sort of sky that might have cleared by eleven or might as easily have turned to rain. But once he got outdoors he felt that expectancy in the air that told him there was a shower to come. When he came back in to breakfast he made a point of tapping the barometer again, just in case.

The girl was making Japanese tea. Jonny had brought Japanese tea for her from London. It had a different smell from any other tea.

It looks better this morning, his mother said to him.

There'll be rain later.

Oh, I didn't hear the forecast.

Well, we'll see how it goes. Perhaps it won't rain after all.

Claire put his eggs before him, toast in a toast rack beside the teapot.

He took up his knife and fork, glancing up at the girl as he began to eat. And what are you doing today?

I don't know. Her bright morning smile. I think Jonathan has a plan to go somewhere. Ely, I think.

That's nice.

It was raining by the time they left. The rain came suddenly, without a change in the sky. Claire told them to take an umbrella but Jonny was optimistic. Jonny never listened to him. Thanks, Mum, he said, but it's only a shower. It won't last.

I wouldn't be too sure about that, Richard said.

The shower grew heavy and the long horizons closed

in. They drove, quiet as the grey outside. Jonathan broke the silence. He's right, damn it. Trust a farmer to know the weather.

Windscreen wipers, limp hedges, blurred fields. Somewhere along the way they passed a combine stopped in the wheat, only a stripe cut into the crop behind it. Some farmer had tried to get out before the rain but had been driven in when he had barely started. He drove on through the fens, long straight roads on embankments and deep dykes beside them. Sharp turns where you didn't expect them, whose logic, he explained, was not to do with the lie of the land or the direction of the road but the system of dykes that you couldn't see.

Ely loomed from a long way off. The town had once been an island, he said, before the fens were drained. All of this orderly farmland they were driving through had once been marshes. It had been a wild place of rebels and outlaws, but then engineers were brought from Holland to reclaim the land.

But it looks like an island now, she said. You could imagine sailing there, sailing up to it in a boat.

For a brief time the rain held off. The sky became luminous, layers of cloud tearing apart. He stopped the car and got out to take pictures. The town with its great cathedral stood out like an atoll above the shimmering grey flat.

Now I think that you are right to use black-and-white. The gaps in the sky closed and the rain redoubled.

Ely was beautiful but the rain went on for too long. It rained off and on all of that week. If you like cathedrals, he said, we'll see some more. So they went to Peterborough, which was not such a pretty town, and spoke about going all the way to Lincoln. They drove for miles and visited the cathedrals in the rain, and Jonathan took pictures. It was a pity, Jonathan said, that she could not see them with sunlight on them, with light inside, how the light transformed them. It was a pity for his pictures. Almost the only pictures he took were of the exteriors, where the rain some days stained the stone black and other days dissolved it into cloud. Claire came with them the day they went to Cambridge, and they saw King's College Chapel, and there the sun came out at last so Kumiko understood what he meant about the light, how light could make stone seem so insubstantial. Richard might have come with them that day but he preferred to stay home. Why, they had said, what can you do there, it's raining, or even if the rain were to stop and the sun come out, it would still be too wet for work. But he did not come. He had to wait for the land or the wheat, one or the other, or both – of course, she understood, he must have needed it to be both – to dry, and he stayed home for the waiting, as if nothing would dry out if he wasn't there. It might have been superstition but he did not believe in superstition. She thought it was just that he needed to watch. He could not bear to look away.

To Claire it seemed that the day without rain had removed a pressure from the house. Or perhaps it was only that she had been outside of it, in Cambridge all day, or that they could be outside now, with the evening sky clear above the trees.

The garden was green and soft after all that rain. There were still deadheads on the roses. Some of the shrub roses didn't drop their petals when the flowers finished, but kept them like ugly brown rags. She would get on to those tomorrow. There were others that might still be flowering if the rain had not got into the buds, though sometimes the damage was only superficial; if she gently peeled off the outer petals that had tightened on them like a brown skin she might still save the flower beneath.

Each year when it came to this time she felt the loss of June. The garden had peaked though the summer had barely begun. She started to think of the next year, how she would make it different for that one, find hot bright flowers for July – and yet she never did, or she planted them without love because they weren't her kind of plants, and they didn't thrive, and the disappointment came again.

Summer wasn't hers. It was theirs, the men's. It happened out there beyond the borders and the trees and the hedges, out in the fields.

I thought we might eat outside this evening, now it's dry at last. It's so nice out. What do you think? We might lay the table out here. We're having such a simple supper anyway, as we were out all day. Some of that ham from yesterday, and these last beans. And mint, there's mint in the herb garden.

The girl nodded but didn't answer. Claire thought that she had spent much of her life saying these trivial kinds of things that required no answer. She had been brought up to do that, to believe that such talk had a purpose, that it was a kind of oil a woman offered to the lives of the people around her that smoothed the days. But what kind of purpose was that, when there was nothing at the end to show for it but only what hadn't happened, the frictions and breakages that had never occurred, that might not have occurred anyway?

She took the girl with her and they picked the last of the broad beans. Sat at the garden table to shell them.

Just a few left. Enough for tonight.

It was easy, sitting there with the girl. There was the companionship and the clean smell of the beans, the satisfaction of breaking them open, slipping her thumb down the cool velvet linings.

Only a simple supper, I put the potatoes to bake half an hour ago.

Richard came out and sat himself down at the table. He was dirty, straight off the farm. His hands were oily from some machine he must have been fixing.

The rain stopped, Kumiko said. And the sun came out. You should have come with us.

He had come straight off the farm, dirty, his hair ruffled, his sleeves rolled up. What did you do all day? Kumiko said. Were you only watching your wheat? She spoke lightly as if it were a joke, what he did. I found something to do, he said. Didn't she know, there was always something to do on a farm? He asked how the fields had looked on their drive. Were other farmers' fields as wet and beaten as his? Had it rained as much around Cambridge? Were there any harvesters out? Just one, Kumiko said, but it was stopped in the field. Or maybe that wasn't today. Maybe it was on some other day they saw the stranded combine, she suddenly wasn't quite sure, all these days and drives had become so much the same. But yes, she said, it had been just as wet there as here. Ah well, that's something, he said. And then he went in.

They had the beans almost done now. Claire held the colander to the edge of the table and with the side of her hand pushed into it the torn green remnants of the pods.

Richard had never been much of a talker. She had thought that was a part of his being so practical. Even as a small boy, when he talked it was always about practical things. His questions were plain – what's that called, or how does it go, not why – and once he had the name of the thing he could store the name and there was no need to say more, was there, because a thing that was named was fixed if not understood? He didn't tell stories. He left the stories to his brother. He just saw, with his clear blue eyes, and named. And he played at making things. It was his little brother who played with words. She hadn't noticed the silence until later, when he came home from school. But that was standard, wasn't it? It was a stage, one thought. Boys went into a silence and then grew out of it. Only Richard's silence came back now and then, heavy and awkward at times as his hands. She had seen his hands there, dirty, awkward before the girl, how he had reached to pick up a bean but dropped it as if suddenly aware of the dirt on them.

Her own fingers were black from the aphids that had infested the plants. It was always the last beans that got the blackfly. Too late now for them to do much harm.

Do you know, she said to the girl, I sometimes used to think that I should have taken us all away, after Charlie died. We might have gone to London, or anywhere. But then they got older, and we were here, and in the summer their friends came. They filled the house with friends, Jonny particularly had lots of friends. I'd come into the garden at night, sit where we're sitting now, and look back at the lit windows with the lights on, knowing they were inside, and think that it was all right. I don't know if it was. If I had done that, it might have been better for us all.

Then there would have been no farm for Richard, the girl said.

No, there wouldn't, would there?

She did not know what it was about this girl that made one tell her such things. She had some quality that affected them all. Sometimes one almost forgot that she was Japanese.

Nothing to be done until there was a bit of wind. Or there were things to be done, on a farm there were always things to be done, but not the things that most needed to be done. After heavy rain, suitable drying conditions were required. Sun. A breeze at least. Not these doldrums. When there was warmth without wind the humidity just hung in the crop. Wind was what he needed, to move the moisture from the soil and from stalks and from the air. It was almost August. They should have been going by now. In past years they had the winter barley in by now. Some years they were well on with the wheat. One year they were all done by the fifteenth. The men's voices echoed in the new barn. They had it all clean and ready, bins cleaned, all swept out. They had never had the place so ready, or so empty. The structure was an industrial one, none of the beauty to it of the old cart barn that had been there before, breeze blocks and steel, roof of asbestos sheets. A hard grey space, doors open, waiting to be filled. The concrete floor of the yard outside it swept almost as clean as the inside. The combine had been ready to go for two weeks now. The tractor stood alongside, the washed grain cart at the back of it. All his machines in order.

The land lay sullen. The green of the trees had deepened as the summer had progressed, heavy now, dead to his eye, even the gold of the fields heavy beneath a drab sky. No light, no movement there, not a hair of the barley twitching, but only the swallows skimming above the crop. There were dozens of them, swallows and swifts, you could not tell how many because your eye could not follow any individual long enough as they swooped and rose and turned and swooped back across one another, but only almost see the pattern of arcs they made that broke the sodden air, and hear the high whistling calls. There was a field of winter barley close by the house. In places it had been flattened by the rain but the combine should be able to pick up most of that. The ripe heads had brackled some time before, bent back against the stems, darkening and drooping now with the damp in them. If they were left much longer and if the rain continued there would be new green here as a second germination set in, the grains sprouting even as the crop stood. He walked on to inspect the wheat in the next field. That too was ready, dense even at the headland. The yield on this field would be good, the price good, if only he could take it now. And get it dry.

The twenty-seventh of July, a full day of rain. The twenty-eighth, the same. The twenty-ninth, only a shower, and so on till the end of the month. The first few days of August began dull and threatened rain but kept dry and brightened towards the afternoons. Four dry days, but the following night it rained. He thought he heard the rain in the night and when he woke in the morning he went straight away to the window. The sky was cloudless but the ground looked wet. The ground mattered as much as the sky. He tapped the barometer on the way downstairs. Went to measure the rainfall in the gauge in the yard. Enough to hold them back a day or two further.

How many days before it's dry enough to start? Jonny asked.

Depends, he said. Two or three. If we don't get another shower.

And then, to get the crop in? Jonny should have known enough about the vagaries of farming to know that you could never predict a thing like that, but he was asking anyway.

Why? You doing something? Need to fix a date or something?

I talked to Jackson this morning in the village. He thought they might get the combine out tomorrow, get going then.

Jackson's always a bit quick off the mark. I don't expect anybody else'll be going yet.

The girl was dressed for sunshine. She had on a little red-and-white skirt and long earrings, with her hair pulled back. He didn't know why she had to dress up so when she was out here in the country.

It's beautiful now, your English August, she said. Now that the rain has stopped.

The sun was shining now, the sky quite blue.

August in Japan is just too too hot and humid, she said. You don't want to do anything or go anywhere.

Then you won't catch me in Japan, he said. He had no interest in Japan, except as this girl made him aware of it.

He could not have had Richard's patience. Even though it was a heavy, reluctant kind of patience, made of dragging the days through, precisely recording each morning the previous day's rainfall. When do we start, he had asked. He knew before he asked the question that it was one that Richard couldn't be expected to answer. But time suddenly mattered to him. In the weeks until then, time had not seemed to matter. Now it did, seeing her wake, dress, go outside, as if with each day that went by something might be lost.

Did she care that the weather was holding them there? That days were passing in which they might have gone somewhere else. Alone, just them, being themselves. If she was unhappy she did not show it.

Such a perfect morning, she said, putting on her sunglasses and hitching up her skirt, which was short enough anyway, to stretch out her legs in the sun.

Let's go straight to Paris, he said. When the harvest is over. You said you wanted to go to Paris. He sat down in the chair beside her, put his hands behind his head and closed his eyes to feel the warmth. Then we can think where to go next.

Can we go to that garden your mother talked about? Is it still there, that garden, where Joséphine planted her roses?

I don't know. I don't know where it is, I'll ask her. But the roses will be finished there too, won't they, if they're finished here.

And if it's rained there like it's rained here, and if any of the flowers are left, they'll be ruined by now. Perhaps we shall go somewhere else.

He opened his eyes and looked about. His mother was gardening. She complained how the weeds grew in the wet. The weeds hadn't stopped growing all summer.

He saw her bent double over the flower beds, throwing weeds to the back of her on the lawn. Then standing, putting a hand to her stiffened back, but she looked happy because she had work to do, satisfied at the fresh heap of green. All of his life she had been doing that, gardening, standing, putting her hand to her back just in that way. As if she would go on like that for ever. So much tougher than she looked.

Shall I go and help her, do you think? Will she like me to help?

Why not? Though you're not exactly dressed for it.

She took up the rake and raked all the weeds and took them in her arms and lifted them into the barrow. It made her feel a part of the place, doing that. Just for that time, no longer. Because she was always outside of it. And them.

Claire had a song in her head while she worked that was the song of the pigeons in the trees. A slow summer song that came back and was constant in all the summers that passed. That made all the summers one single summer in this place. From his deckchair Jonny was watching. He used to watch from the walnut tree – or was that Richard, who used to watch up there? The tree was old now, the lower branches gone, no good for climbing any more.

Why don't you pick us some raspberries, instead of just sitting watching others work?

When the girl had filled the barrow she went with Jonny. Claire didn't mind. She was used to working alone. When she worked alone her thoughts disappeared into the work for whole stretches of time in which there was only the touch and the smell of the leaves and the soil, the sensations of the here and now and nothing before – or of all the time that had gone before held in the here and now.

The two of them looked happy together, so far as she could see. Was that a good thing or not? Would it mean that this girl would take him away? And how would it be, for whichever one of them it was, to live one's life elsewhere, with someone from elsewhere? What would they say to one other as time went on, day to day, in a marriage? In a marriage, did people understand one another more or less as time went on?

The swifts arced across the lawn. She knew they were there by their screaming calls, even if she did not look up to see them. There were not so many other birds to hear this late in the year, apart from the pigeons. The pigeons persisted all through the day in the trees about the garden, their cooing passing from one tree to another. Even in August the flutter of their mating persisted in the foliage of the wisteria where they had their nests, hatched halves of white eggs to be found on the grass below all through the summer and into the autumn if the autumn was mild. The sound of the pigeons seemed to her like a drug, repeating as if time did not exist, from when daylight began until it ended. Almost, she felt as she worked, that the sound was inside her. It had been so all these years she had lived here. She had lived every summer against the sound of the pigeons. Lulled year on year. Looking down to the plants, to her hands on the soil. Not looking up but knowing the creak of their wings as they flew overhead.

When she went indoors to make lunch she experienced the silence there as a sudden loss. It seemed strange to her, that all this had been here, all of the day. That all this was really so. This old dim house. The sitting room whose open door she passed, lit green from the leaves of the wisteria that hung down over the windows. These rooms, this table, these chairs. These cups by the sink.

In the corner of her eye she saw Richard coming back across the yard. Even now there were times that she mistook him for another man – or if not mistook, then remembered the other man in him. He was so like him in his walk, and much the same age that he had been when they came here and took on the farm. Dogged like him, or maybe it was the work that made them that. It was such material work, this dealing with soil and machines, with plain intractable things, the results of it all there before the eyes. All so tangible. (And yet she remembered that Charlie had a dream in him once, or was it just his youth? She did not know if Richard ever had a dream.)

It had been at this time of the year that she had first realised that she was pregnant with him and yet even the having of a child had seemed only a possibility – not tangible, only a flimsy idea, herself flimsy beside the solid fact of the farm, so that for days she had moved about with the secret gathering weight inside her, moving as she did now, slow, weeding to the sound of the pigeons, moving in and out of the house, sleeping under the weight in the afternoons, not telling until the harvest was almost done, as if she inhabited a world less real than Charlie's. The harvest was much further on that year, the fields around them already stubble. They were walking in the evening across the stubble when she told him, the sound of some other combine still going on a neighbouring farm and the cloud of it in the distance. I think I'm pregnant, she had said, reaching for his hand,

and he took her in his dusty arms, his shirt smelling of sweat and grain. (And even then was his own possibility there in him, his own secret withheld, the dark embryo of what was to come?) And now here was she, and her two sons, and Charlie long gone, and wheat out there once more waiting to be cut. Putting the thoughts away, living day to day. No pain. Only the present task.

So many raspberries, the two of them had picked. They wouldn't last. They would go mouldy too soon with the moisture. She would have to pack some for the freezer if she wanted to save them.

By the time they sat down to lunch the clouds were closing in. It looked like it would rain again.

Did you hear the forecast today?

No.

It's almost one, time for the news. I'll put the radio on.

The forecast came before the news. Scattered showers, sometimes heavy.

Well, we might have told them that.

She spooned the raspberries from a bowl. Summer there in the glass bowl, and a spatter of rain on the window.

What shall I do now, one or other of the boys would say on days like this. When it was wet outside and when the holidays were long. Or at the beginning, when they first came home, when there was the sense of the days stretching empty before them and they had been so busy at school. The emptiness must have hit them when they came home. They ran about in it and called it freedom but acted as if they were trapped. They ran wildly through the house, bowling imaginary balls with windmilling arms. How about making one of those model aeroplanes Uncle Peter gave you, she would say. I don't think you've made them yet. But sit still, indoors; how could they do that? They were too wild to sit still. She was angry with them for being in the house, though she had longed to have them home, their urgency pressing on her like the weight of the day outside. Angry as if they were prisoners together, in this echoing house which was home, with the lovely garden outside bounded by the hedges that she herself had planted, and the wide empty spaces beyond.

When this brief shower ended she would go out into the garden again, however wet it was. She would kneel on a pad placed on the wet grass and tear at the weeds, which were lush and came out with the wet soil clinging to their roots, and the process of it would calm her, the seeking of the weeds among the plants, the touch of them in her fingers, and at last she would rake up the green mess into the barrow and wheel it to the compost heap that smelled of grass and decay. But as the afternoon went on the sky would clear. The evening might again be fine. These past few evenings had tended to be clear, with always in them the hope of a dry day to follow. Before she went indoors she would go back around the garden, looking at where she had worked and where there was work yet to be done, inspecting buds of whatever was flowering and breaking off deadheads between her muddied fingers.

Burying Billy

He was fourteen or so, home from his public school. The boys went to different schools now and it set them apart from each other. They didn't even come home on the same day. Jonny came first. He was already settled in by the time Richard came back. Jonny was lucky in that there were boys his age in the village. There didn't seem to be any of Richard's age around.

Can I go shooting with Billy?

I suppose so. If he says that's all right.

Maybe it was what he needed. She'd let them have air rifles but they hadn't up till then done any more shooting than that. She'd let Billy keep Charlie's guns for them. She might have got rid of them altogether but she hadn't. It had been a part of staying on, carrying on the life that Charlie had left.

Billy wasn't to be put off by a boy's silence. Billy didn't speak that much himself.

They walked out side by side. The youth was far taller than the man, and the man's coat was too long for him, reaching almost to his knees. It was still one of Charlie's old coats that he wore, an old green waxed jacket – she would never have thought it could have been kept so long, old when she had given it to him, worn and torn after all these years, and shiny with the wear. Possibly Billy had shrunk in that time. His hair was quite white now beneath his cap and he had grown a grey fuzz of beard. His old black Lab, Rosie, walked at their heels, slow now, she too grey at the mouth. She saw the three of them coming back, Richard carrying a hare, its two hind legs tied with string, his hand holding the legs and the string, putting it down on the old mounting block in the yard behind the kitchen. Not speaking. The hare had been a big one so its head hung down off the edge of the block, awkward and staring. Had they talked at all? Billy didn't enter the house. He turned away, nodding goodbye, with Rosie lagging at his heels. C'mon, old girl, was all she heard him say. You could see Rosie wouldn't be walking with Billy much longer. When the old dog died, she thought, Billy would be alone.

How was it? she asked, when Richard had taken off his boots and come in the kitchen.

We got a hare. His look was bright but exhausted.

I thought you were after rabbits.

Billy says rabbits aren't sport any more. They're all myxy, the rabbits. Dying of disease whether you shoot them or not. Had a shot at a woodcock though.

The brightness was there under his words but he wasn't showing it to her. He went past her and poured a glass of water, drank it where he stood.

It was nice of Billy to take you.

Yeah.

Perhaps he'll take you again.

Serious now, glass put down. A tone of voice that indicated he was about to ask her something. But, Mum,

Rosie's getting old. Billy says the vet says she might have to be put down. Can I take Jess with me next time?

That's a good idea.

When Rosie dies, will Billy get another dog?

I don't know. Maybe he'll think he's too old to get a young dog.

If he got one and he died, then we could look after it, couldn't we? I could tell him that. Then he'd feel OK about getting one.

Well yes, I suppose so.

After that he went out with Billy and Rosie and Jess, and then only with Jess.

When Rosie finally died – not at the vet's but at home, where Billy wanted her to die – he said he'd help dig her a grave.

That's kind, she said. She had never seen him so kind to anyone.

Can we put her out on the farm?

So long as you don't get in Jackson's way.

I thought we could put her somewhere they used to shoot. I thought of a good place.

Yes, that's fine.

He took a spade to dig the grave, and the old man came with the dead black dog slung like a shot deer across his shoulders – still strong, he must have been, for all that he had shrunk – and they walked out into the fields. When they came back Richard went into the workshop to make a cross. He worked on the cross for a few days. They were quiet days because Jonny was away somewhere, staying with a school friend. Just herself and Richard in the house, and he calm and industrious. He found some pieces of oak, put them together with a joint which he had learnt in his carpentry class, not nailed but joined, and he planed and varnished it, and then he carved on it the dog's name, and a little lower down, the year it was, 1963.

How old was Rosie, Mum?

I don't know. You'd better check with Billy.

So he found out how old she was and then he carved the year of her birth above the year of her death. He made it quite beautifully.

There wasn't time for Billy to get another dog.

He got ill during the next term when the boys were away at school. She didn't tell Richard how ill Billy was. He was an old man living alone. Sometimes anyway one didn't see him for days. Nobody in the village quite realised how ill Billy was until the ambulance came. He died just before the term ended.

You should have told me. I could have come home to see him. I wanted to see him. You never let me see things.

At least he was home for the funeral. It was astonishing how full the church was. You didn't know Billy could have had so many friends. They came in old cars and vans and on bicycles, and some of them looked as if they had come out of the past, rural faces of a kind that you thought you didn't see any more, scrubbed and shaved for the occasion, arriving early and shuffling in, filling the pews from the back first. When she came in with the boys there was only space at the front. She and Jonny walked on up the aisle but Richard peeled off and squeezed himself in at the back. It was the first funeral they had been to. They had been too young, she had thought at the time, to see their father buried – you didn't want children to see that sort of thing, they thought in those days, it was all too horrid for them, too much of a shock. But the boys were older now, not children any more, looking older and stilted and unlike themselves in their school suits. The light was bright in the church that day. It was a winter's day but the low sun was streaming in at an angle across the aisle. She looked round when they were singing. The light from the high windows fell hard on the faces of the old men in the pews behind. It struck their bald heads and their whiskers and the lines on their faces and their gnarled hands. Richard stood out among them, a public schoolboy, tall and young and straight in the black suit which she could see was already becoming too small for him, hair so golden in the light, thick and golden and sticking up on his head where it didn't brush down, his face smooth beside all those weathered ones, pink, cheeks shining with tears. She realised how he had loved the old man. She could see his mouth mouthing the words of the hymn but she wasn't sure if he made a sound. She could see his shining face but she couldn't distinguish his voice from the rest. There might have been a glass wall between them, she and Jonny at the front of the church, Richard and the old boys where the cold light shafted onto their pews at the back. He looked so tall – he was very lanky just then, before he filled out – the school suit too short in the arms, his long wrists bared and his hands so large holding the red hymnal. Why had he chosen to sep-arate himself? She had thought the three of them should have sat together. Suddenly she saw that they were apart. It only showed now. They always had been apart, even when they had seemed together. Perhaps they had been apart from the beginning, but it was only later, looking back, that memory told her that. Or perhaps memory made it so, hindsight paving the way for the present. If you were a mother you looked back again and again, attempting to explain how it was now, seeing moments when it might have been different, if you had made it different then.

Looks like we'll be able to go at last.

Go? The word confused her. Where were they going? They were not going anywhere. It was the combine that was to be going, the beginning of harvest. Later she would think that it was also the beginning of going. The beginning of the end of being becalmed.

Looks like we'll be able to go.

She had drawn the curtain. The day was bright. No clouds. Jonathan spoke from the bed, sitting up, yawning at the sky.

We'll be on the move now. Thank goodness for that. I'm sorry, I've kept you here too long.

Last night's dew was heavy, Richard said. We can get the combine out there but we can't start till lunchtime. We'll have to wait for the damp to clear.

Claire was happy at the sound of their voices as they walked out into the yard. Men's voices, her two sons' voices mixing with the voices of the other men, the purpose in them of the work they were about to do. This place of waiting filled all of a sudden with purpose. The sound of the machines starting up. The tractors and the combine. The combine having to be driven out to where they would begin, readied in the field.

Jonathan hadn't driven a tractor since that summer before he went away. He felt the past judder beneath him. The blue scent of it in his nostrils.

Concealed in the oaks at the edge of the field the pigeons went on calling. A few white puffs of cloud grew in the sky. When they made their start Claire went out with the girl to watch. One year spilled back into another, the circle rounded, ends joined. Richard was suddenly animated, flowing. Doing what his father did. Maybe all the solutions were there, in the work, in the plain growing of things. That all that mattered.

Richard climbed up to his seat in the combine. From the high seat he could see far across the land. He could see to the end of his fields and across the fields beyond, see the rising dust where other combines worked in the distance, see the village and the church tower, and another church in the village beyond. He set the header going, its long blades moving. He began to work forward into the grain, the revolving header like a great yellow wheel cutting into the sea. The machine roared beneath him. It chopped up the sea.

When the combine was full Jonathan drove up alongside. Kumiko watched as he positioned the cart directly beneath the spout, adjusted his speed to match that of the combine. Then he put a thumb up to Richard and Richard let the grain go from the spout. It was good to see. The grain spilled down, a golden stream into the cart, dust rising about it. They had handkerchiefs tied over their faces because of the dust. They drove alongside one another, aligned, brother to brother, until the flow of grain ceased. And when the cart was full Jonathan would drive it back to the yard and unload, and return to the field before he was needed for the next load.

In these days nothing was missing. Everyone was present. They were golden harvest days. Her boys were men. One year spilled back into another. The years when they did not have the farm slipped out of sight, as if Richard had after all taken over directly from his father. As if Charlie had been there to teach him, Charlie still present in all of them. She would turn and go back towards the house, and there would be the sound of the machines sure behind her, the combine in the field, the tractor driving between the field and the yard, the other men in the yard working the grain as it came in.

Now he was driving in a sand-coloured cloud across the field in front of the house. The wheat was coming in thick onto the turning reel of the header. The wheat in this field was dense. The yield right across the farm looked good this year, and in this field in particular. Though there was still more moisture in the grain than he would have liked.

All that was needed was another few days of sun.

Then this harvest would be all right after all.

Jackson – no, not Jackson, it was his son Tom who was doing the work now – was out on the neighbouring farm. Farther off, she could see others at work, the dust of other combines moving in the distance. Richard had taken off his shirt in the heat. By the time he came in he would be red with sunburn.

Want a ride? he said. You can ride up with me for a bit. He was taking a break. The tank was full and the grain cart was still out at the yard. She climbed the metal ladder and perched beside him holding the rail. It was hot and dusty. Jonathan came out with the tractor and stopped alongside. Both machines stationary this time, Richard pulled the lever to let the grain go. She held a hand over her face against the choking dust. Thumbs up. No talking, the machines were too loud for speech. Jonathan moved the tractor away. Richard set the header turning again. The combine moved forward into the wheat. She looked down to see the stalks drawn in and churning across the cutting blades. It was different up there, above it all. Looking out and down at the field ahead, the cut stripes where the combine had been, the rest of the crop waiting, the tractor away at the side, waiting. A long view out over the flat land. A sense, with the roar and movement of the great machine, of being on the bridge of a ship going out into the ocean. But the element in which they moved was wheat, not water, and already her skin itched with the dust. Richard drove the length of the field, turned about, worked back, turned again. She didn't know when he would stop. They didn't speak. Though he was so close they could have spoken only by shouting. When the combine was full again, Jonathan came again and drove alongside and took the grain, and Kumiko watched and the combine didn't stop. She put her hand to Richard's arm and he paused long enough to let her climb down. When she walked back through the cut field the stubble scratched her bare ankles.

Little brother was doing OK. Possibly a bit slow. Slower than the others would have been, but it seemed a good thing to have his brother doing the work and not some outside hand. Every few loads Jonny fell behind and there was a delay as the combine had to wait for him. He might have asked one of the other men to take over but he knew that Jonny was keen to do the job. And there hadn't been anything broken yet, and no spills. One expected a novice to break a thing or two at harvest. Though he wasn't really a novice of course.

A smile passed between the brothers along with the thumbs up.

Well done, Jonny, you did all right, Jonny. That's what the thumbs up meant. They called him Jonny as if he was still their boy. And he smiled a boy's open smile. He was happy just then. She could see that. He was in his place and he was proud. Maybe this was his place after all, he should be here always. But this was only a moment of sunlight. It was the middle of the day when the sun was up in the sky, everything bright, no shadows to be seen. When the moment passed that boy would have secrets, like boys do. Things he hid in pockets, at the back of his drawers. In his memory. That separated him from his brother. That separated each of them from the other.

He had been going nine hours. It was hard to stop after so many hours. It had been getting dark for some time. He had seen the sun setting behind the village. He had seen the last of the colour fade from the sky, put on the headlamps, but their light would not be strong enough to keep him going very long. He would like to have driven on until it grew quite dark, on and on in an industrial process, his mind narrowed in a tunnel of light. He kept his eyes concentrated now on the strip he was cutting, the sight of the wheat falling before him, which was no longer so smooth now but thrashing and lumping. His hearing was all for the sound of the machine, the constant of the engine, the dull roar of the drum. He heard as the dew began to fall. The stalks were becoming moist, beginning to slip against the blades. The rhythm was beginning to slip, bundles forming and breaking, the straw lumping and beginning to jam. It was tempting to keep going, to try to finish the field, or this stretch of it at least. He drove more slowly, attending to the machine, to the sound deepening and becoming erratic. If only he might keep at it, finish the strip, finish the field, work on through the night as if the rest of the world had fallen away. There would be only what loomed up before the combine, and the following tractor, its lights also on now, that moved away and then back alongside – and in other fields in the distance, the pattern repeated by other men. Tom Jackson was still going. Old Jackson would be out there with his son, watching, listening, with all his half-century of experience, stepping down to put his hand to the stalks; holding the decision to himself. He would not go in before the Jacksons. When Tom Jackson went in, then he would too. He would go in tired, his eyes stinging and his muscles aching, the throb still in his body, the reverberation in his head. He would eat and bathe, and sleep black sleep, and as he fell into that sleep the heads of wheat would still be falling and churning before his eyes.

He would sleep long and wake late. It would be later than he was used to waking, the day bright outside, a fully formed summer's day, the others up before him, breakfast cooked, bacon waiting in the oven. Jonathan would already have been in the yard, and the girl out there with him, and the men; the concrete swept and the grain in the store piled high. Time to service the combine for the next day's work. Wait again for the dew to lift.

For a week the harvest went well, then the weather turned against him. A single day of heavy showers meant that it was too wet to work for some days afterwards. Morning and evening, Richard went out to walk the fields that hadn't yet been cut. On the third day he went out alone and got the combine started, in the field where he had left off, just to see how it was, but he had not gone far before he felt the weight of the machine begin to sink into the wet ground. Once more he stopped, and left it out there. He hoped that it would not sink deeper before he could get it going again.

All it took was another day of showers for the pattern of waiting to be repeated.

The swallows flew ever lower over the lawn as if the air pressed them down in the arc of their flight. There must have been swarms of insects there in the humid band of air close to the ground where the birds swooped to feast. Claire heard them close overhead as she moved about her plants. The soil was almost too wet to work now. And besides, the growing season was almost over. There was really no need to weed any more in August, except for tidiness. The look of things.

When she was done with weeding she stood and stretched her back. The sky was grey but she thought it had infinitesimally lifted. The insects must have risen. The birds were flying higher.

Jonathan and Kumiko had walked to the village and were making their way back. They too watched the swallows, skimming low above the standing crop. Some of the birds seemed to fly no more than a wing's breadth above the heads of grain. But others were gathering on the telegraph wires ready for the summer to end. Jonathan had thought they would themselves be finished and gone long before the swallows. Now he wondered if the swallows would be gone first. This was something he could not bear about farming, being the captive of the weather and the place. He was not steady like his brother. He could not have had his pragmatism.

Another two days of waiting and then Richard thought they might try again. The combine was stuck and they needed the two tractors to pull it out. It was a waste of precious dry time. They pulled it out, and got going, and had just managed to finish the field they were on and set up on the next one before a fine rain came spitting down from the sky, at first no more than pinpricks of cool out of the sultry air. They went for the headland, trusting to their luck. Once the headland was done, the field cut all around its circumference, there would at least be room for the wind to enter and dry out the heart of the crop. They worked without pause. They could see that it was worse for others. In the sky to the south they could see the darker grey spill of a heavy shower elsewhere. They kept going as long as they could, until the rain was measurable and the stalks too damp. The next day they held off, and the next one they went out again, and it continued on like that through towards the end of August. They worked in snatches, going for what crop they could take. What was left in the fields flattened further with each storm and grew dark with the wet.

———

They were in the kitchen having breakfast when Richard came in.

Here, look at this. Richard placed a head of wheat in her hand. Among the grains was what appeared to be another grain, only black and elongated and misshapen, like a dried mouse dropping but attached to the stalk.

What is it?

It's ergot.

It looks evil, she said.

Nothing evil. Just a fungus.

What does it mean?

It means, I'll have trouble selling the wheat. It's a bugger, that's all.

Let me see, said Jonathan.

This, too, he could not bear about farming, the way that a problem could strike, quite out of your control. His brother had come in and made the air in the kitchen heavy with this problem that was in no way of his own making.

Can you do anything about it? he asked.

Stupid question. Richard just threw him a look.

All the same, even at a time like this, there was something he envied. There was something so solid, real, about Richard and his work. Where Richard was concerned, when things went wrong his failures took material form, even when they were so small as an infected grain.

What was a photograph beside that? Only a notion. A stain on light-sensitive paper. Give it too much light and it disappears. And a photographer, making a living as some artsy photographer; that seemed fantasy. Childish, in this world of men.

Even his brother's physical presence seemed more real and purposeful than his own, his tall figure that dominated the room and made the women look at him. If he were to take a photograph of that, it would show: the domestic scene, the big handsome man entering from the outside, in motion, his fair hair caught in the shaft of light into which he walked, the seated women looking up; a second man, smaller, dark, seated away towards the edge of the frame, no more than an observer.

Richard pulled back a chair and took up the mug of tea his mother offered. He wasn't going to waste words. He had told them all that it was necessary to tell. The frustration of this moment and of all this harvest was there in his face and in the scrape of the chair. Kumiko examined the infected grain a moment more and then put the head of wheat down, fastidiously, on the cloth beside her plate.

He felt a sudden regret that he had brought her here, into his past, perhaps that he had come back at all. You would have thought that some years away would have changed things; that their relative positions would have altered when he returned. But here he was again, holding back, watching. Not their fault, but his own. No one had made him sit in this particular chair but he was sitting in the same chair where he had always sat, on the far side of the table, closest to the window. So often he had turned the chair just a little when he sat here, leant his elbow on the table and looked out through the window instead of into the room.

And he was doing that now, looking out at the familiar view, the cobbles, a portion of the yard beyond which the new barns weren't visible, the old stables, the cars parked there – it was the cars that changed more than anything, that would have fixed the date to any picture or memory of that view – hearing his mother saying with a touch of brightness, Just sit down a minute, exactly as he must have heard her say it a thousand times before. I'm sure it's not all lost. I'm sure it won't be that bad, just wait, sit down, I'll pour you a cup of tea.

His mother knew as well as he did that if Richard was angry, he had to act. Do something. Take the anger and use it to fuel some other action. That was what he had always done. Don't think about it any more, just do something. Go outside. Get on your bike. Climb a tree. Throw a stone. Break pots. Smash your mother's greenhouse. They did that once when something was wrong. Richard's idea – not that it was ever spoken, but only done. Richard had led him there and begun it. He didn't even know if Richard had thought the thought before the first pot hit the ground. And he had followed because he did. Because he too understood what was wrong and because smashing things seemed to right it, the sound, the shattering terracotta, the spilled black soil.

This problem was nothing compared with that other one. This was a material problem from Richard's material world. And not so very terrible, when it came down to it. Action was simple. You scraped the chair back and sat down and drank your tea, then slammed the mug on the table and pushed the chair back again, and went out to the barn and checked again the grain that you had already brought in, to reassure yourself that that grain at least, that you had brought in earlier from other fields, was all right, free of the fungus, that that grain would sell all right, get a good price; and your brother went with you because really, despite the differences, he wanted to help. So they did that. Then they went out later in the day and cut the headland of that last field, even though there was probably too much moisture in it. There was no point in doing any more. They packed up after that and went in, and because he still couldn't rest, Richard suggested that after supper they might go out lamping.

What's lamping? Kumiko said.

I'm not sure it's your sort of thing, Jonathan said. He wasn't sure it was his either, not any more. So why did he say he'd go? Old times' sake. Richard's momentum. Because rabbits were a pest and this was the best moment to get them. Because they were brothers and lamping was fun.

Going with them felt like a dare. She liked the feeling of going with the brothers, doing what they did, being the third, the girl in the men's world. They waited until it was dark and then they went out. It was very black outside, no moon or stars. The farm was very quiet, out all alone in the countryside. It was one of those nights when the rest of the world didn't seem to exist.

The night was dark, the cloud cover making it unusually warm. The scent of the tobacco plants drifted across the lawn. They were flowers for the blind, that you saw all the better when you closed your eyes. Claire heard the shots from the field. They must be getting a lot of rabbits. In all the time she had lived with them, husband and sons, she hadn't come to understand why men so liked to kill things.

First Jonathan driving, then they would change places. The canvas roof of the Land Rover rolled back, Richard standing with the shotgun and leaning against the roof of the cab. The field naked, the rabbits exposed, which had lived and bred all summer hidden within the crop. Where the rabbits showed, like rocks strewn on the bare land, the Land Rover drove fast and directly towards them and Richard fired. The rocks moved. They moved fast but the Land Rover was fast, bumping over the stubble, skidding on the turns because of the slipperiness of the cut straw. They ran from its lights but at the same time they were caught in them. They kept to the beams as if the beams were tunnels from which they could not escape, and only now and then did one by sense or accident veer off out of the beam and into the safety of the darkness alongside it. The gun fired, reloaded, fired again. The rabbits fell. Some of them fell directly, simply folding or rolling over in the beam. Others were wounded, and the Land Rover slowed or diverged then from its path to follow the erratic animal for the gun to finish it off. Why had he said he would do this? It was Richard's game, not his. So often he had found himself playing Richard's game.

A slug of whisky from the hip flask they had brought out with them. A switching of roles. The man on the roof rapped on it when he was ready, and the driver drove. They shouted to one another through the window over the noise of the engine. Left. Straight ahead. Go for it. Left, left. Hold on tight while I turn. Yeah, that's great. Get that one. Good shot. Jonathan shot well. Perhaps he shot better than Richard that night, or perhaps that was because Richard drove better, more evenly and matching his speed to that of the rabbits. They told Kumiko to count but she lost count after twenty. She seemed to enjoy it, shouting out too, holding on to the door beside her and to the metal frame of the cab, as the Land Rover lurched across the fields. They must have shot dozens of rabbits. A good night's work. Passing the hip flask. Driving back, all three of them in the cab now, Kumiko in the middle seat and the brothers on either side. All three elated. But Richard driving slowly now, all settling back into their separate grown-up selves.

When they got to the yard the clouds had opened up and let through a slip of moonlight. Kumiko stayed out alone. She wanted to feel the night. Calm herself. See some stars. She had never done any kind of hunting before.

As the clouds broke further apart and moved away, she thought how they would begin to show, the bodies on the ground.

Richard was beside her. She didn't know where he came from. I was just going to lock up, he said, then I saw you. I nearly locked you out.

Will you go and pick up the bodies tomorrow?

No, Richard said. Something will scavenge them. They'll be gone soon enough.

She said she didn't like thinking that.

It's how things are, he said. Nature is hard. We used to have a word for things like that, Jonathan and me, 'maumau'.

I know, she said. He told me once. (Only Jonathan had been talking about more than nature. He had been talking about men, what men do to men, what he himself had seen, what he could not erase.) But it's funny, she said. We have a word in Japanese that sounds almost the same, '*mā mā*', but it means something very ordinary, sort of OK. Nothing bad at all.

He was standing close so that she could feel him beside her.

The nature I know is not so hard, she said.

No, he said. That's what I like about you.

She turned. She felt the pull of him and she turned. Kissed him then in the dark when they could not see one another. Like they were nameless. Not themselves.

Then they drew apart. She could not have said who moved first. There was only the darkness then. Nothing spoken.

She left him without a word and went into the house. Undressed and got into the bed beside Jonathan. She thought that he was asleep, but he wasn't. Or he had been asleep, and woke when she came in. He stirred and reached for her, put an exploring hand between her legs. Often they used to make love like that, so easily, before they slept. But you're already wet, he murmured, with a kind of surprise. With a half-asleep chuckle in his voice that she wouldn't forget. Ready for me, he said. And slipped into her in an instant.

Then he was asleep again, and she lay awake for hours. She heard the clock in the church across the fields, pictured the rabbits lying there on the ground. It was not right, not ordinary, not OK at all.

She slept very little that night. Soon after it got light she went out. She crept downstairs as silently as she could and unbolted the door, and the dog woke and came out with her.

It was where the summer led, she told herself later. Something that they had been waiting for, in all those sultry days in the countryside, that was growing in them when they had thought they had been waiting only for the harvest. Like the fungus, growing in those conditions and fastening on the head of wheat. She had learned a bit about ergot since then. It caused hallucinations. There had been times in history when ergot had got into the harvest and into the flour, and when the flour was baked into bread its effect was so powerful that whole villages went crazy. There was a theory that it happened in a place called Salem when there was a witch fever. Women became hysterical, and others saw strange things and blamed the women who they said were witches. And then the women were burnt at the stake. She didn't know where Salem was, when she first read that. She imagined it must be some village on its own in the marshes, like the villages she passed through with Jonathan when they drove to Ely, but it wasn't anywhere like that. It was in America.

Or maybe it was something in the spinney. The old witch Richard said lived there once. She might have left some evil behind her.

But no. It was something much simpler.

She got up and went out because she simply could not be in that room any more, with Jonathan's breath on her shoulder; shifting carefully so that she did not wake him, going to the window, drawing back the curtain just so much so that there was light in the room to dress by, looking out and seeing no one. It was early. Too early even for Richard to be up. She felt better once she was out in the morning air. There was the sound of the pigeons. The dog for company. There was a heavy dew, almost a mist, spiders' webs made visible on the grass and on the stubble where they were coated with the dew. Untouched.

———————

He saw the dog first. Someone had opened the door and let her out. Then he saw Kumiko. He ran to catch up.

You're out early.

You know that I always wake early.

All these mornings he had seen her but had not spoken of it. But you don't come outside, he said, panting, slowing his pace to hers. Away from them, in the house behind the tall hedge, the curtains on the spare-room window were only half drawn.

This morning I thought I would.

It's almost September. Almost autumn.

There was a milky sheen of dew over the ground. That was why when he had seen her in the distance she had seemed to be walking so smoothly. As if she was floating. The air above was clear. Even where they breathed it, the air was clear. It was going to be a fine day, finer and bluer than any just passed.

It's good to be out so early, she said.

But she looked sleepy, as if she hadn't slept well and needed to go back and sleep some more. She looked like she had just thrown on her jeans and T-shirt and hadn't brushed her hair. Not so neat as usual. As he looked at her and thought that, she put her fingers through her hair to smooth it out, put up both hands to twist it into a knot. But what are you doing here, she said. She raised her head so that the knot slipped a little.

What I usually do, he said. Thinking what should be done. Her hair was heavy, he thought. He could imagine the dark weight of it in his fingers. No, not imagine. He had felt it the night before. Were they pretending the night before hadn't happened?

Look at the spiders' webs, she said.

The webs made all the surface of the field glisten. There were bales piled here and there, rectangular bales in regular square towers. Where the combine had most recently cut, the straw still lay loose in its rows, where it had not been baled before the rain and must be left to dry for some days after. In the far field before the spinney most of the crop was still standing.

I have to think when we should get out and finish that field, he said. With all this dew it'll take the longer to dry. Though it'll hardly be worth the effort.

Why's that? she said.

Because of the ergot.

Oh yes. It was clear that she had forgotten the ergot.

He thought by the tone of her voice, what I say doesn't matter. She's not interested in whatever I can think of to say. Definitely, they were pretending.

There were big birds flying up from the stubble where

they had been the night before. Buzzards, Richard said. They had been feeding on the dead rabbits. There were crows on the field also, but they stayed on the ground and didn't fly up.

People didn't like carrion birds, Richard said. People didn't see that they had a purpose and kept the place clean.

There were skylarks overhead. Climbing in the pale air, beginning to sing. Should he talk to her about the skylarks? That would have been a nicer thing to talk about. Why was it that skylarks climbed in stages? Had he not noticed that before? Or had he always noticed it, known it, and only thought about it now because she was here with him? Because she was from outside, and made him see things differently. The spiders' webs. The birds. Up the larks went to some level, and then they held there and sang, and then they climbed again, level by level, until they were lost to the eye. He was going to get someone out to plough the stubble next week. His mother said that he shouldn't, because of the skylarks. She said that the skylarks needed the stubble to live in through the winter. But he had told her they seemed to do well enough.

See how blue the sky is now, Kumiko was saying.

Yes, it'll be a fine day.

They were close to the spinney.

Come this way, come here. Let me show you something.

Perhaps they weren't pretending any more. There used to be a house here, he said, taking her hand just so lightly and leading her in between the trees. He knew a way in that wasn't too overgrown with nettles. He held back branches so that she could pass. Not skylarks over them now but rooks, rising, circling, cawing. There was an old chap who used to work for us, Billy, who remembered when the house was here, when he was a boy, and there was a woman still living in it. We used to think she must have been a witch. Look, this is where it was, you can just about see the foundations.

She did not say that she knew the place already. They had met him there before, on the track, but he must have forgotten that. They had been in the little wood, and when they came out Richard was driving by in the Land Rover, so handsome and casual with his elbow on the open window, and stopped and picked them up, and Richard had said that he still went shooting there, and Jonathan thought that he didn't care. As if it was just a little wood where they shot pigeons and there once used to be a house. An innocent-enough place.

There was hardly anything left of the house, just some lines of brick and rubble in a clearing, a pit and a broken slab of slate with runnels in it that had been a draining board. It showed up better in winter when the undergrowth died back, when you might find bits of rubbish, old bottles and things, about the place. Once he had found a clay pipe. Would that be interesting to her? What should he say? What were they doing here together, pretending? It was early in the morning and they were hidden away in this little wood with only the birds and the dog to see them, and the dog had disappeared off into the undergrowth. He might say what he liked, just for this moment. As if they were only playing, only themselves to see or hear, out so early while the rest of the world slept. He didn't dare touch her. Not yet. He talked instead. That made the moment longer. He told her how he used to come with Billy, when Billy put feed out for the pheasants. Billy liked to give the pheasants a little bit of grain, to draw them over from the shooting estates, from Jackson's where the syndicate got young pheasants in every year for the sport. Pity Billy wasn't around any more. She would never have known anyone like Billy. He told her about Billy, how Billy would talk. He mimicked old Billy. He used to be good at mimicking Billy, when they were boys. Now he did it again, shrinking and hunching over like Billy, pulling at the imaginary cap on his head, making her smile. She was standing where the sunlight fell on her between the trees, smiling. Her house was just here, boy, see. Old lady like a witch, we was scared of her, us youngsters. I remember coming to this door here, just here it was, and the garden, you can see where she had her garden, the pear tree there, and the well. Privy that way. Weren't no bathroom o' course. And when old Hannah died the house was let be. Falling apart good enough as it was. No point going and modernising an old house like that, was there, boy, out in the fields with no electric or water?

Now she was laughing. Moving between the light and the shadow. He thought of Billy taking a moment's rest on the broken brick wall after walking out here with the bag of grain for the pheasants, his whiskery face and watery eyes. Billy in his father's old coat. He told her how she would have liked to have met him.

Richard talked more than she had ever heard him talk before. He made her laugh. She had not seen him like that, so light-hearted, before.

More solemnly he told her how they had buried Billy's dog. Rosie, her name was. Over there, he said. I made a cross. It's probably still there if we look.

Then he stopped talking. As if he couldn't think of any more to say. The rooks were loud overhead. His hands hung very still at his sides.

Something in your hair. A twig. There, it's gone.
Her hair was heavy and black, falling away, the knot already unravelled.

His hand was more delicate than she would have thought such a hand could be, a hand that dealt with big rough things, with machines, but so light just then that she wasn't even sure it touched her. She put up her own hand to his. She might have just moved it away, gently, tactfully, just put it away, so that he had taken whatever it was that was caught in her hair and it would have been gone, and all of that moment might have been delicately put away.

Her hand small in his. Her touch soft, and dry. Holding, stalling, his. Movement stalled.

She might have slipped away, out from the trees and into

the fields. And when they were outside of that wood, where almost no one ever went anyway, where they would never have needed to go again, then the moment might have been left behind there in the tangle. They would have been out in the clear fields and the daylight where things like that were not allowed to happen. Only she did not slip away. He did what he should not have done. And she did what she should not have done. Because Richard had been somehow at the heart of all that summer, since she saw him that first morning out there in the wheat when it was still green. They were standing under the tree. He reached to her hair and she put up her hand to move his away, and he caught her hand in his. She had her back to the trunk of the great tree. He held one of her hands in his, and put his other hand to the tree beside her. He was the summer. He, they, the two of them, were destroying the summer. She spoke too late.

This is crazy. We cannot do this. I should not be here. Why did I come here?

She spoke softly, her hand twisting in his, but holding it all the same. She could have gone. She could so easily have gone, twisted away, but she did not move. She only spoke, in that soft voice of hers. We can't. Can't what? Whispered words. A racket of rooks overhead. But she had begun it. She had come out to find him, hadn't she?

Can't. Can't. The rooks had all the words, over their heads. Nature is hard, he had said. The bark of the tree hard on her back. Rooks black in the morning sky. His eyes open and blue. No shadow in them. Like sky. Why no shadow? Can't. And not there. Not with what had happened there in the past.

Something bad had happened there in the past, but something bad was happening in the present. She saw that she was the one who was doing it. She was suddenly aware, and angry. His eyes looking into hers. So blue. No shadow in them. Did she want to see shadow in them, before she could move? Or was it only that she could not pull herself away?

No, she whispered. The rooks were loud above them. No, Richard, we can't do this.

How could you do this? she said. And here, why here? How could you bring me here, of all places?

She could feel the confusion beginning in him, his body stiffening, eyes looking about as if there was something that he should have seen.

You know, don't you? Here. It was just here. Right here on the ground where we're standing. Jonathan knows. Jonathan saw. Jonathan told me.

She was talking out loud now. When she had started to speak it had been only a whisper. She did not move. She did not pull herself away. She went on, aloud, becoming cruel. Driving the point home. Wanting him at the same time. It was a kind of violence.

But you must have known, Jonathan always knew, everyone knew, only they didn't say, because you people don't talk about that sort of thing.

What, what thing? he was asking.

Again he asked. He was beginning to understand. He was letting go of her, drawing back, turning away to look about him at the place where it had happened. But he had to have her make it plain. So it was all clear. So that he knew what Jonathan knew. No more secrets. So

207

that was what she did.

And then you buried that dog here. What made you do that? Don't you see what that meant?

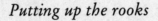

Putting up the rooks

Suddenly she was sorry. She put those neat little hands up before her mouth. Like a doll surprised.

There was no way she could take it back. She had said what she had said, and everything fell into a new place.

It all made sense.

He dropped his arm from the tree. Nothing could happen here any more. Something had happened here once in the past and now there was no present to be had here. Only the past. He let her go, without a word, hands held to her face but in shame now, careless of the nettles that brushed against her jeans and her bare elbows as she went. Even she had known.

He used to come with his father and shoot, just here. Not when it was green like now, with the leaves and the nettles, but in winter when it was all brown, the ground and the trees. Shhh, Richard, his father would say, and he would stand beside him, still as the dog knew to be still, not right under the oak where Kumiko had pointed but at the edge of its cover where there was a view out onto open fields and sky and the pigeons coming in to roost. He had stood in this spot beside his father until he had grown cold, and his mind drifted so that the pigeons always surprised him when they came. But not his father. His father raised the gun and fired, one, two barrels. When a bird fell the pleasure of it warmed them.

One barrel only, it must have been. Here. Somewhere about here. The pigeons flying up, and the small birds out of the bushes, and the rooks from their colony high in the trees. Had the birds flown up in astonishment, at a man who shot at himself?

He could not understand why he had not thought it before. (Or no, he might have thought it but dismissed the thought. Who wants to dismiss a truth they have believed since the age of ten? Or a lie, rather.) The story as she told it fitted together. It was so much more likely, when you thought about it, than any accident. Here, it had happened; planned, executed, not any accidental incompetent cocked-gun tripping over some fence. A man out in the early morning, come for the purpose, dying here.

He shouted then. It was neither a word nor a scream but only a twisted cry. Damn. Damn that girl, damn them all. Was she too far off to hear it? The sound stretched and melded with that of the hundred rooks that he had set rising and cawing over the trees.

He looked up where the black birds whirled under the sky. Light up there. Sunlight, seeping down. The nettles a bright green where the light struck through them. He stumbled out where the girl had gone, not following, only going out into the light, away from this place.

The house was plain to see. He wasn't going into the house. The Land Rover was in the yard. The keys hung on a hook in the barn. He got into it and drove. He drove past his fields, bare stubble open to that sky, out from the farm to the village, and through the village, and on, until he was on some road that he did not know – or perhaps he knew it but no longer recognised it because so much in him had changed – driving through land that was strange to him though the look of it was the same as the land he had left: wide flat land, acres of stubble interspersed with fields of glossy green beet. It was other men's land, and it meant nothing to him. On some farms they were so far ahead that they were already burning the straw. On one he saw a tractor beginning to plough. There were others – and these were more – where there was still wheat left standing, or where the rain had hit particularly hard, harder than at home, and swathes of crop had been flattened to the ground. He thought these things automatically, and the thoughts dulled him. The Land Rover was slow, heavy to drive, its interior bare, nothing to muffle the noise of the diesel engine. It smelled of diesel. He wound down the window and rested his elbow on the edge of it as he drove. A low green car passed him, too fast and dangerously on the narrow road. A Sprite, but he barely noticed it. He wanted a cigarette. He didn't have any cigarettes on him or money to buy them. Then he saw that the tank was low. If there was no money for cigarettes then there was no money for diesel. He stopped in a lay-by, scrabbled about the vehicle, amongst the clutter in the shelf beside the dashboard, on the floor and between the seats, for loose notes and coins, and found what amounted to a couple of pounds. The next petrol station he came to, he put in a meagre gallon, watching the dial. That's all I've got, he said to the girl on the forecourt, counting the change out into her hand. He had held back enough for a packet of fags. He didn't pass any shops after that, not until he got to the village. He stopped outside the post office and bought a packet of ten. Then he broke it open and sat in the stationary vehicle and smoked, looking down the street at the houses, the Green, the church beyond it, the few cars passing.

So everyone knew, did they? Jonathan knew. His mother knew. That girl had known, and she was no one, a stranger over the other side of the world. Perhaps he had always been aware that there was something that Jonny had seen that he wouldn't tell. But that was Jonny's way. Jonny always had that way of looking like he knew something you didn't. Jonny hid things from you and sometimes he told you stories, and you knew you wouldn't be able to tell when a thing was true and when it wasn't.

He wasn't like Jonny. He didn't have anything hidden. He saw what he saw, a plain world, and that was what he knew, and if he didn't see for himself then he believed what his mother said, even if he didn't believe what Jonny said. Even when it was a lie.

They would be there at home waiting for him. What would the girl have told them? Most likely she hadn't told them anything. They might think something had happened between him and the girl, but if they thought that then what they thought would be wrong – mostly at least. Sooner or later he would have to face them. He put the cigarette almost finished to his lips and held it there as he started the engine. Took a last hard drag and threw it out the window. No, he might stop at the churchyard first, just up there beyond the Green. Park before it, go in the wooden gate to where the grass had been freshly mown about the graves. See his father's name there on the stone.

He didn't know what difference it made. He already knew that a steady man was not steady. He had known that since he was a boy. A big steady man could disappear in a puff of smoke. Ever since he'd known that, his father's death had been more important than his father's life, than whoever, whatever, his father had been. So, if the manner of his death was different, what had changed? If the past changed, did that change the present? There was the smell of mown grass, a path between dark yews that stood like raised hands against the sky. The name on the stone was the same name. He thought there was a rule in the church that suicides might not be buried on consecrated ground. Then there had been a lie here also – or a kind blind eye.

He remembered how they had come to the door, Billy with the dog, the policeman, the other men. They knew because they had found him. There was old Billy's grave, over in the corner. He had come to Billy's funeral if not his father's. He remembered Billy's pals all around him, old men with weathered faces standing there beside him singing 'The Old Rugged Cross'. Did they all know? He thought they did. They must have known. And Billy was buried here in the churchyard, and his father was. Rosie they buried in the spinney where his father might have been buried, in the leaf mould where the nettles grew up, so green when the leaves caught the sunlight. That had been his idea, to bury Rosie there, not Billy's. Perhaps he had sensed there was some meaning in the place, and Billy went along with it, knowing what the meaning was. Yes, boy, that'll be a good spot for her, she'll like that, you know we used to go shooting there, when your father was alive, it was a good spot, your father was fond of that spot, you'll remember that. To Billy it might have made some kind of memorial.

He thought of that first time Billy took him out shooting. How he shot the hare – so great it had been to get a hare his first time out with Billy – and how Billy did not congratulate him but only said, That's it, boy, now carry it home and you'll see what hares are made of. He carried the hare all the way from Hewitt's Field, and learned how heavy it was, the dead weight of it that he could feel again, pulling down his arms.

At last he turned away and drove the mile back to the farm. He went up the drive and parked the Land Rover in the yard. They would all be having lunch by now. They would be waiting for him. When he came in they would see him and, whatever they thought had gone on this morning – unless the girl had told all of it, and he thought that surely she could not have said it all – they would think they knew who he was. They would be sure of him as he had been sure of the memory of his father. Only he couldn't be sure of any of them any more, of his mother, or Jonny, or old Billy whom he had trusted so completely. Good shot, boy, you'll be growing up like your father, you will. You'll be running that there farm in no time.

Claire saw her come in. She walked past her. She did not tell her anything. She went straight upstairs, and Jonathan followed her up and she told him that she had to go. Go where? he said. I don't know, she said. London, for a start. She was packing already, taking things out from the drawers and the wardrobe. He said, It's Richard, isn't it, and she said, No, yes, but it's not what you think, it's not just that, although that was a part of it, it was something else, something I said that I should not have said, you will never forgive me. I told him, Jonathan, I did not know that he did not know.

That was not quite true. And Jonathan knew it was not true. He did not say. He only looked at her. She was taking her clothes from the wardrobe and folding them and putting them in her case. He left the room.

She packed everything. All her clothes, folded in the case, except for the clean ones she would wear. Then she went to the bathroom and washed, and gathered up her bottles and things, and brushed her hair, hard, and even put on some make-up, though she didn't usually do that in the mornings. She took her case downstairs. She wanted to be gone before Richard returned, persuading Jonathan to take her to the station, saying that she would talk to him later, in London, in a day or two when he came, if he came, to see her.

When she got to London it was raining. She realised she had left her raincoat hanging by the back door. It did not matter. She could buy an umbrella easily enough.

———

She had taken a liking to the girl. But she was a foreign girl, from a long way off; from Japan, after all. She had been bound to leave, sooner or later. And now she had. That was what visitors did. Visitors came and stayed awhile, and then they left. The girl had come in flustered this morning and run upstairs, and when she came down again she looked very neat and clean, contained and Japanese once more, her suitcase packed and placed beside her. She noticed too late that the girl had left her red raincoat behind. She ran out with it just as the car turned away down the drive, hoping Jonny might see in his mirror and stop. Not to worry, she thought. He could take it to her sometime, couldn't he?

The trip to the station and back took an hour at least. She spent the morning waiting for one or other of her sons to come home. She made soup for lunch and laid the table for the three of them. When Jonny came in he saw the table and asked if Richard was back. No, she said, but I thought I heard him coming into the yard. I laid for the two of you.

───────

He slammed the door of the Land Rover, went in the back door, down the little corridor to the kitchen. They were sitting at the table having lunch like on any ordinary day, the two of them sipping soup and a place at the end of the table laid for the girl perhaps – or perhaps it was laid for him, as if he had just been out on the farm and was coming in a little bit late. There would be a bowl warm on the Aga, soup kept warm for whichever one of them it was. Such an everyday scene, except for the fact that one place was missing, and you did not know which of them it was who was meant to have been there. The two of them looking at him, spoons raised. Sunlight coming in the window over the sink, where a flypaper ugly with trapped flies dangled and shuddered in the draught.

His mother started to get up to bring him some soup. No, don't do that, I'm not eating. He walked out and on to the office. He took the key from the central drawer of his desk and opened the metal gun case in a cubby-hole to the side of the room. He took out a shotgun and a couple of cartridges and went out again, by the front door this time so that he did not have to pass them.

I'll go after him, Jonny said, running to the front door.

No. She pictured horror. No. Not you. You can't. She caught him back. If anyone goes, it has to be me.

They tussled on the step there for a moment and then he saw that she was right, and let her go, and she ran out down the drive, hectic, apron flapping. She was still wearing the blue apron she had been wearing to cook, that she had been too distracted to take off before lunch. But already Richard had disappeared from view, down the drive, past the hedges. He might have turned in any direction after that. The hedges hid everything beyond.

Come back in, he said. It'll be all right. She was walking back so slowly, taking off the apron as she walked, smoothing her hair, closing her eyes and opening them as if to dispel a dream. Come inside and sit down, I'll make some coffee. He'll be all right, you know Richard. He'll settle down. He always does. It'll be all right, you'll see.

The kitchen was quiet. A fly buzzing on the fly paper. The kettle coming to the boil. They heard a single shot in the distance. Claire stood. Jonny turned to her. The shot – if it had indeed been a shot, and not just some sudden bang, or bird-scarer (but what bird-scarer could there have been this time of year?) or backfire – was not repeated. The fly buzzed. He took the boiling kettle off the heat.

We have to go, she said. Both of us.

Yes. Only when they moved it seemed they moved so slowly.

They saw him coming back up the drive. Upright, striding, the gun under his arm, a tall blond man like a hunter coming home. He looked to them where they stood at the door of the house.

That scared you, didn't it?

They looked shocked, the two of them, Claire and Jonny, the two of them always alike and most alike now, with that same expression on their two scared faces. He knew what shocked them. They were seeing a ghost. He knew them so well, and this narrow little world that they lived in. He placed the gun down inside the door and walked into the kitchen. They followed him, not speaking. There were the two soup bowls on the table, the third place that they had laid, and a fourth chair unused, with no place before it, that might have been laid for someone else, if someone else had been there. For the Japanese girl, but the Japanese girl for some reason was nowhere to be seen. Then for his father. That was who it should have been for. And he wasn't there either. He was gone too. And now he knew how he was gone, and he knew that he was a different father than the one he had been before. Because his father was only his death. That was the thing about his father that mattered more than anything else, that had made them what they were. They were cowards, all of them, shutting themselves away here in this house, closed away with the wide flat land around them.

Fire

She didn't see Jonathan in London. She couldn't tele-
phone to the house because she was afraid who would
answer. She wrote to him instead, and then she waited
a number of days but he sent only a brief note, that he
would not come. Maybe one day, he said. Not yet. Maybe
better in Japan, not here. She knew what he meant by
that. She did not expect him. So she left on the first flight
she could get. It was with a Scandinavian airline, flying
north to Helsinki and then across the Arctic. (Funny,
she thought, it was not such a great distance as people
might expect, that way, to get from England to Japan;
the earth was round, after all. So maybe he wouldn't
be so far away as it seemed, not always, not for ever.)
The plane left from Heathrow and looped about over
London, and then took a course north and east over
the countryside until it reached the sea. It might have
flown over Norfolk. Over the farm, for all she knew.
She watched from her window at the edge of the wing.
She understood now the patterns of the fields. Green
pasture. Golden stubble. Brown plough. Fields where
stubble was being burned off: a flickering line of orange
flame, thick smoke spilling away, spilling out flat and
white across shiny, newly blackened land. She saw that

there must have been wind down there, driving the fire. Richard had spoken about the danger in that, how a single burning straw might carry fire from one field to another. How a farmer must look to the wind before burning the stubble, to take care that the hedges would not catch; that to be safe he must first plough a firebreak of bare soil around the circumference of the field. She hoped that the hedges were not burning.

There was something Jonathan had told her, when they were still in Tokyo, that he said he had to tell her before he left. She had thought that he was telling her something she should know before she could go to see him in England, if she was to go and see him in England. That was where he went wrong, she thought. It wasn't her he needed to tell. Not she who should have been the one to know.

It was the last weekend before he left Tokyo. He was doing his packing, in his two-room apartment in Inokashira. He had packed in a big case all his envelopes and yellow boxes of photographs, and put beside it the black metal boxes of equipment. His camera was still out, and his few clothes, which he could stuff into a rucksack later. There really weren't many clothes, she was always trying to take him shopping to buy him more – just a few T-shirts and jeans, and two pairs of shoes, one to wear and one to pack. His nice leather jacket, that he had bought when he first came to Japan, he would wear. Come and see me in England. Please say that you'll come soon. Come in the spring. But she had said that she couldn't get a holiday in the spring, not long enough to go to England. In the summer I'll try, she said. She had been thinking only of a holiday then, not thinking then that she might quit her job and go for longer. And then he told her. He'd never told anyone else, he said, but he needed to tell her. He needed to speak the words. For himself.

He said that his father had killed himself. That no one said that, openly. It was said that it was a shooting accident. Except it wasn't easy to accidentally shoot yourself dead with a shotgun. And in England it was a crime then. Suicide was a crime in those days, a shame, unspeakable. Maybe that was why people didn't say, or maybe they didn't say out of kindness, but they did say things about how his father was moody, how he had never been quite the same since he had come back from the war, though the war had been a long time earlier. They didn't say it, but he knew what they thought.

How do you know it wasn't an accident?

I know because I saw.

You saw him do it?

I was there just after. Where he was. I woke up early and saw him go out with his gun. And I thought I'd go out too, and I found him.

When he said that she couldn't touch him. He was standing across the room, just looking and not seeing her, as if he was in a different place. And then he turned round, mechanically as if he had switched himself on again, and slid back the doors of the high cupboard behind him, reaching in to get something out of the back of it. She loved him very much just then. She wanted to go across and touch him but she couldn't. He was so determinedly looking away. That was how he was. When he was in pain no one could touch him.

His voice was very clear, as if he was speaking a poem or something, not speaking to her, a girl across a room, or as if he was speaking out loud to himself because inside he was deaf. When my mother told us, she said something different. I knew that what she said was wrong because she said he was in a different place. She just made up a story. To protect us, I guess. And the story is still there. We all go along with it.

Later, in bed, in the dark, with whatever wasn't yet packed scattered on the floor around them, and the two of them sleepless, she had asked him, Why did you tell me that?

I think I just wanted to tell someone, before I could go home.

So you've done it. You can go now.

Yes, he said, I can. And you must come and see me there.

But he had said what he said for himself and not for her. And what he said next made her a little afraid to go. I think my mother blames it on the war, he said, like people do. That he had a terrible time in the war.

Well, people did, didn't they?

What?

Have a terrible time.

Yes.

And they brought it home with them.

Yes.

I don't think it was only the war, he said then. I think it was more complicated than that. But it's easiest to say, isn't it? And turning to her, his head close, his hands about her hair. My mum might find it strange that you're Japanese. Don't worry though, she's all right, my mum, she'll like you, you'll see.

And your brother?

He'll like you too.

Perhaps they all three liked her for coming from outside.

She slept on the plane, and woke and thought of the house burning. She looked down and there was only

Siberia, vast and bare, and the shining wing of the plane. She saw the house on fire down there, flames leaping from old long-dry timber, beams, floors, furniture, the flames so bright and the smoke so thick that it could not fail to be seen, however high the plane flew. And she saw the three of them, tiny smoke-blackened figures running out from the flames. Like the figures in the photos Jonathan once showed her. It suddenly seemed like arson, what she had done.

ACKNOWLEDGEMENTS

So many thanks, on this book and always, to a constantly wonderful team of editor and agent, Alexandra Pringle and Victoria Hobbs, for their thoughtfulness and faith in my work. Also to the rest at Bloomsbury, to Mary Tomlinson, and Jessica Sinyor at A M Heath. And to the farmers, David, Tom and Nell.

A NOTE ON THE TYPE

The text of this book is set in Linotype Stempel Garamond, a version of Garamond adapted and first used by the Stempel foundry in 1924. It is one of several versions of Garamond based on the designs of Claude Garamond. It is thought that Garamond based his font on Bembo, cut in 1495 by Francesco Griffo in collaboration with the Italian printer Aldus Manutius. Garamond types were first used in books printed in Paris around 1532. Many of the present-day versions of this type are based on the *Typi Academiae* of Jean Jannon cut in Sedan in 1615.

Claude Garamond was born in Paris in 1480. He learned how to cut type from his father and by the age of fifteen he was able to fashion steel punches the size of a pica with great precision. At the age of sixty he was commissioned by King Francis I to design a Greek alphabet, and for this he was given the honourable title of royal type founder. He died in 1561.